Underlying Conditions
Pangyrus 9

Composition by Esther Weeks
Cover design by Doug Woodhouse
Founding Editor: Greg Harris
Managing Editor: Amanda Lewis
Asst. Managing Editor: Yelena Chzhen
Fiction Editors: Anne Bernays, Virginia Pye
Assoc. Fiction Editor: Indu S. Guzman
Poetry Editor: Cheryl Clark Vermeulen
Assoc. Poetry Editor: Cynthia Bargar
Nonfiction Editor: Artress White
Assoc. Nonfiction Editor: Aime Card
Zest! Editor: Deborah Norkin
Schooled Editors: Christelle Saintis, Michaela Gaziano
In Sickness & In Health Editor: Erica Reaves
Field Notes Editor: Rachel West
Comics Editor: Dan Mazur
Columns Editor: Apratim Gautam
Graphic & Web Designer: Esther Weeks
Editorial Assistants: Tessa Rudolph, Saffron Forsberg
Title from Julia Lisella's "*The New York Times* Publishes 1,000 Names"

Pangyrus
2592 Massachusetts Ave #2
Cambridge, MA 02140
pangyrus.com

Contents

Nonfiction

Poetry

Underlying Conditions
Pangyrus 9

Note from the Editor

Grief does not have five stages. Grief is the collapse of your formerly level world into a fractured mountainscape. It's flood and fire, earthquake and avalanche.

That doesn't mean the five stages are not real. They're just not what they pretend to be, science. They're an image in words. A sketched-in staircase, to hold onto when a thousand things, seen and unseen, threaten to pitch you lower. When you panic that there's no bottom, there's no world of *after* you can believe in the way you believed in the world of *before.*

They're poetry.

So, too, "Underlying Conditions," the title of this volume. Conditions are conditions; they get named underlying when a collapse is in view, when the surface has dropped—is dropping—threatens to drop—away, and we need to know why.

When the artists in this volume started writing, Ukraine was uninvaded. No Supreme Court Justice's wife's texts to a presidential chief of staff had yet come to light. Germany still eagerly lined up the mouths of its natural gas pipelines toward Russia. Omicron and its variants had not yet begun to wave.

And yet the news in these pages is fresh, the images in words are ones you can hold onto. This is the power of our written art. To paraphrase Aristotle: history tells you only what happened to occur. Poetry tells you what *must* occur.

Given underlying conditions.

Some of the work here grapples directly with the questions of what we face. "Can Your House Kill You?" Amber Wong asks, unfolding a story of her work with the EPA, the painstaking science and engineering at a public agency trying to protect people from an invisible toxin. This time it's people in Tumwater, Washington, but it could be any of us, dealing with any of the many threats that lurk unseen, that require trust in such agencies.

Some take the literal and twist it literary, such as the poem that gives this volume its title, Julia Lisella's "The New York Times Publishes 1000 Names." Our national paper of record, to convey the enormous emotional and human toll of the pandemic, gave over its front page to the names of some of America's fallen. Lisella, armed with poetry, takes on the poet's task—and the reader's reality—that even this shattering list is "only/ a portion of what ails us"…

> This is the virus and that is the gun.
> This is the virus and that is the knee on the neck. This is the
> vigil and that is the vigil…

Our conditions are not all bleak, of course. Angie Chatman, in "Ode to Pound Cake," connects memory and recipe, a family history of slavery and her grandmother's devotion to the Black church, to arrive at the beauty of a seasoned soul, a seasoned pan: "By eye and by hand the nicks and cracks are present on the outside. The inside is smooth and supple, honed by years of use."

Over and over in this work is the encounter with the essential human conundrum: what are we, and what are we to each other? In "Alone," poet Jonathan Andrew Perez begins his meditation on police abuse of power, "From childhood, on Pitkin and Easton Avenue, I have not been/ As others were." In "with what letters remain," Christopher Porcaro observes:

> we sew each other's
> bones to our own
> & pray the graft takes

And in Allison A. deFreese's "Aspiration," we have an image of us perched between threat and wish, the business of everyday life and encounter with fundamental mortality.

> Will you drown
> while waiting to fly
> to save time

Above all, we need to be open to the strangeness of things, on guard against the deadening assumptions that our assumptions will hold. In "The Battle of Silicon Valley at Daybreak," Alexandria Peary imagines emojis at war "in a countryside green as a dollar bill."

Tim Weed's "The Tawny-Green Steppe" gives us the figure of a Darwin whose scientific-imperialist investigations in South America are accompanied by "the presentiment of a devastating truth dwelling just beneath the surface of articulated thought. The dread feeling that there will be no containing it, no reconciling it, no putting it back in its rightful place."

In "Animal Instincts," Melissa Mulvihill's routine walk with her dog turns into a discovery of just how deeply our bodies and minds are imprinted with the long struggle of our species to survive. In Lindsay Leigh's "Folklore" series, images of "real and imagined customs and superstitions" occupy a surreal space where culture and wishfulness, fear and conviction, experience and imagination collide. Or collude.

Perhaps the essence of this art of ours, the weaving of stories against the threat of uncertainty, is summed up by Jacqueline Houton, in "Tasseography": "there is something sad and beautiful about a big-brained animal that

sees symbols in random stimuli, that assigns names to arbitrary arrangements of stars, that looks for truth in the bottom of a teacup."

That beauty is here.

We have so many people to thank for putting this issue together. Esther
Weeks, our web designer from the very first hiccup and cry Pangyrus made
at its online birth, brought her skills to the print medium. Amanda Lewis,
our managing editor, wrestled the task to manageable dimensions, then,
together with Yelena Chzhen, managed them. Our excellent editors and
staff consulted on the pieces and copyedited. Doug Woodhouse, our cover
artist, launched a new-for-us style of visual metaphor for the cover. And of
course the authors, our subscribers and donors, the volunteers who keep us
running — we're grateful to all of you and hope, with this bundle of artfully
labored-over paper in your hands, to have done you proud.

    —Greg Harris

In Case of Moths

by Allaire Diamond

For days at the tail end of the Obama administration, I haunted my neighborhood thrift store, casing the free pile and the clothing racks for anything pink. I took it all — shrunken cable-knit cotton pullovers, flowery girls' sweatshirts, a well-worn cardigan in gorgeous lilac wool, its simple design and roomy size rendering it perfect for deconstruction and rebirth.

Drawn to my sewing machine, I used my basic skills to stitch these discarded garments into hopeful, or at least cathartic, pink 'pussyhats' for the 2017 Women's March, and passed them out to anyone who would take one. Forty or so of these hats joined a river of pink flowing toward Vermont's capital on January 22; the interstate highway became a parking lot as over 15,000 people converged on Montpelier. Heads encased in repurposed threads, wrapped in fibers perfectly evolved for strength and warmth, we emerged all together, metamorphosing to flutter haltingly toward some uncertain future.

As spring emerged from that winter's cocoon, I became aware of a distinctive shift in my house. Something new had made a home here. My first reaction to finding several oblong, delicately swollen tubes in my sock drawer was wonder. These tiny structures spun of fine fibers were beautiful, like tree buds. They lay alongside dark brown, perfectly pocked spheres resembling ancient pollen grains cored from a bog, clearly distinct from flecks of dirt or dust. Curious about these newfound works of some tiny craftsman, I continued exploring. I rifled through the rack in my closet — when was the last time I had worn that silk dress or my grandmother's mink coat? Surely not in this decade. From those long-dead minks' lustrous pelts, a tiny pale insect emerged, like a petal caught in a breeze. Wonder mutated into panic.

I compiled a dossier on my awe-inspiring, though not-entirely-welcome housemates. Casemaking clothes moth (*Tinea pellionella*) larvae consume the protein keratin, found only in animal skins and their derivatives – feathers, wool, silk, hair, and leather. These larvae spin tiny, cigar-shaped cocoons, about 3/8 of an inch long, retaining the color of the fiber they've digested. They can spend as little as a month and as long as two and a half years foraging and spinning their cases, in some cases molting, or shedding their soft exoskeletons, up to 45 times. Temperature and food govern their metabolisms — their life cycles accelerate in warmer climates and summer months, and vice versa. A litter of eggs hatches from a toothpaste-y looking smear (laid, for example, on a folded thrift store sweater) at the same time and each larva has similar access to the same food, so the larvae tend to mature and pupate as a cohort, emerging together as adults.

Those discarded cases and frass in my sock drawer were signs of transformation. Adult clothes moths are weak fliers and tiny, eating nothing during their final life stage. They don't seem fleshy, but rather constructed of fiber and powder and dimness themselves, with an uncanny ability to disappear in midair, in the center of a room.

As realization dawned that these tiny insects were inhabiting far-flung corners of my home, I periodically found myself standing as still as I could, trying to detect the flutter of a tiny wing or the telltale isosceles triangle lurking on a wall. I trained my eye to distinguish their awkward flights into the shadows from the light-seeking, stronger flights of the outdoor moth fauna that sometimes ventured inside. Yet often, the clothes moths I knew were there — had just seen! — seemed to render themselves invisible, leaving me powerless and exasperated at my failed peripheral vision.

The fliers I see are almost all male, following chemical pheromone trails emitted by females waiting in dark, soft corners and folds. These airborne males are taking risks (me and my subpar spatial perception) to expose themselves and cross unfamiliar terrain. Meanwhile, their more successful counterparts are already in the drawer, simply crawling down a collar or across a sleeve to meet their mate. Once they mate, eggs safely laid on a delectable bit of forgotten fiber, the parents die.

Clothes moths drummed their faint but steady wingbeats through the ensuing years. I suspect they arrived on that beautiful lilac cardigan that made so many pussyhats, explaining some of the worn patches on the fuzzy wool nap. Friends told me that they were probably here to stay, unless I wanted to mount a dramatic push to wash every single textile in my house (I didn't).

I developed a strategy involving woollens in ziplock bags, expensive European pheromone-coated cardboard hanging in closets, once-worn clothes kept out of drawers until washed, all anchored by the bulwark of an antique cedar chest, which provided ultimate sanctuary for vulnerable natural fibers. I took to periodic bouts of obsessive vacuuming, spraying cedar oil and vinegar on shelves, slow-roasting wool toys and clothing in my oven. In summer, I gratefully anticipated heat waves that could heat my car's trunk to moth-broiling temperatures, and stuffed it with bags of bedding.

Our relationship, the moths' and mine, centered on our mutual yet conflicting desires for the same resources, and we each used our distinctive powers to gain an edge — my hulking size, intel gained from internet as well as actual stalking, and access to a global marketplace containing cedar oil and German cardboard; their surreptitiousness, patience, and exquisite powers of keratin discernment. Despite my wish to see them gone, I felt, sometimes, a strange kinship with these aggravatingly successful creatures, as I began seeing and inhabiting my home through their epidermally-focused senses. I became intensely attuned to animal fibers, mentally mapping my space with woolen landmarks. 'Mothish' things began to draw me: keratin, darkness, dusty stagnant crevices, the need to chew and spin and mate.

It's not entirely clear to me why clothing moths exist. Though larvae feed on proteins associated with animal skins, they thrive only when these external coverings, once providing protection and personality to a living creature, are removed from the animals that made them, tucked away, forgotten, left in the dark. The classic moth habitats, both uncovered in my research and discovered in my home, are patches of dense wool rug beneath a heavy piece of furniture pushed against a wall, or a forgotten knitted mitten, its mate long lost, at the bottom of a box in the basement. Clothes moths seem to have coevolved to some degree with humans, exploiting not just our need to warm our pathetically furless bodies, but also our tendency to accumulate extra garments and store them out of sight.

Two years into my moth cohabitation, I visited a coworker's home, a stately place that feels more Downton Abbey than Bennington. It was built nearly 200 years ago, at the height of Vermont's Merino sheep craze. Donald's wife Margaret raises sheep, creates dyes and spins wool. While showing me her latest projects, she mentioned that she had recently noticed a moth flying out of one of her wool bags. Eager to be helpful, I jumped in ready to share my accumulated storehouse of knowledge, tips, and experience with *Tinea pellionela*. I couldn't imagine the work it took to produce wool and then see that get eaten away. Smiling, she said she had read that moths don't like sunshine, so she had simply decided to keep her wool bag on the windowsill.

Margaret's approach bent my moth mindset forward. I had felt like I always had to be on guard to keep my home from becoming a moth haven. Just one errant wool sock unsealed in a drawer of plant fibers and synthetics could spawn an entire eclipse of moths! At certain crazed moments, I had pondered tossing everything but a tiny basic wardrobe, never storing anything long enough for a moth to alight.

But if dark, stagnant corners and discarded, forgotten layers can breed lives of their own, I'm drawn to the idea that a bit of sunshine and transparency can help me coexist fully in the changing ecosystem of my own home. The starker the boundary I try to place between my own life and the rest of the living, chewing, reproducing, case-spinning world, the more intense the frustration and the more deep the self-delusion.

For now, the moths and I continue our dance of shelter and sustenance, destruction and retreat, guided by our own prerogatives. My sock drawer is still filled with ziplock bags and the moths still show up in surprising new places every couple of months, keeping things interesting. They are here to stay and so am I, trailing cedar vapors and pheromones in our wake.

Schadenfreude

by Romana Iorga

Everything comes at a price.
This evening, too, will have to be
atoned for, somehow.
The balcony door is open
and the dog watches our neighbors
bicker outside. She's wagging her tail.
Who knows, they might look up,
notice how patient she is, how
intensely attuned to their drama,
and the next time we run
into them in the street, they might say
good girl and give her a treat.
This is all happening only inside
my head, of course. The dog's tail
keeps wagging, the balcony door
stays open, the neighbors are loud
and cringy, to use my son's favorite
word, which means we sit
in the dark, silent for once, listening
to other people air their dirty linen.
No use in hiding from the truth.
It feels good. Pleasure at someone
else's misery: a commodity like
any other. We choose to pay and pay
and pay, since sadness is free.
But isn't joy what we pay with?

Isn't sadness what we deserve?
What if we stepped outside
and leaned over the railing. What if
we called them by their names.
Asked them to join us for dinner.
Would they hear us? Would they be
angry, grateful, ashamed? Does it
matter that one quiet evening
we almost shed our undeserved joy
to peel someone's sadness away?

Spiders on the Hancock

by Max Heinegg

Steady at their webs on the brilliant edge, Chicago
spiders range outside the windows
across the 94th floor, at every vantage
their dedicated tensile silks arrayed
upon the beams, a metal of their own.
Is this occupation accident, or do they know
leaders? One pioneer who gathered
the colony for an ingenious monopoly

on the city's Icarian flies? Or squatters
on the palace as the window washers strike,
chanting below, banded for a $5 raise?
When the workers return to their bravery,
will they say, It's you or me to the company,
or send them flying with a Happy trails, Hans?
Even one friendly minds the clutter
of eensy-weensies shrouded on the glass,

but the view's irresistible, so we press on Tilt,
eight bays at time facing the towering facades.
Here is the corporation, & here, individuals
dangled in the overhang, a dotted line of eyes
the horizon signs left to right, from Lake Michigan
to the pinnacles, whose height affords this
hovering interest in such daring creatures,
who dying become lawsuits, beads woven in situ.

Three Micro Stories

by Meg Pokrass and Jeff Friedman

Gifted Sister

My oldest sister is gifted. When things break, she fixes them. Though often they still don't work, our parents beam with pride. Sometimes our gifted sister breaks things just to fix them. And our parents beam with pride even more, except when she breaks things like my father's electric razor or my mother's hand mixer or blow dryer. Our gifted sister causes glasses to spill their juice on my other sister and myself. We are not gifted, but we know when we're thirsty and wet.

There are mysteries we don't understand like why our pet turtle now has a crack in its shell, but the shell still holds together even though the turtle has "fallen asleep"; why we found a trail of tiny slivers of glass sparkling in the carpet; and why our gifted sister smashed our pet plastic amphibians against the linoleum tiles. "Don't worry," she said with great confidence. "I'm taking them to my hospital; they'll need surgery." "What hospital?" we asked. "Shh," she said. "Do you want Mom and Dad to find out?"

Sometimes, for no good reason, our gifted sister hurls a candy dish or a plate against the wall and runs into her room, slamming the door. Then our mother stops our father from going after her. "Wait until the storm dies down," she says. "Then talk to her." Nor do we understand why our gifted sister screams at our father behind a closed door while our father says harshly something that sounds like "Now look…" and then, after much commotion, they come back to the living room together, our gifted sister, still with tears bright in her eyes, kissing everyone on the cheek. Our mother smiles at us with thin, tight lips as if she expects us to smile and swallow at the same time, as if we are all in on the secret of how difficult it must feel to be gifted.

***

Owl Eyes

Her father rescued the owl, nearly dead, tail feathers mutilated. He lived permanently in her backyard in a homemade cage, so tame he was like a sibling, so timid about the world he wouldn't go away even when let out. He perched on the fence and stared at her in a way that no boy had ever done. She knew her father watched over her as if she were also wounded — too vulnerable to leave the house or the yard, even though she was restless and always looking out a window or over the fence at the other houses. He confined her, so she talked to the owl. "It's our secret," she said, knowing her father would not allow it — if he actually heard what she said and saw the love in the owl's eyes. And sometimes the owl glanced at her as if to take hold of her body, as if he saw the fragile bones hidden inside her rough wings, as if he could breathe the delicate air in which she lived.

***

The End of Her Blue Period

When she picks up blue man from a dance rehearsal, she invites him to stay and offers him supper. "I'll pop over to Safeway for red," he says, and he always buys bargain flowers at the register. When he returns, he's holding a bottle of wine without a label and some blue irises that have probably been stolen from someone's garden. "Here, you take these," he says, "and I'll put on some music." And it's just at that moment, she realizes that his blue eyes are not really blue, and his wan face reminds her of cold oatmeal. Still, the room brightens from his irises. She lives in a gray apartment building sandwiched between two smelly parking lots. She painted her walls off-white, but the off-white has turned grayish with the smoke and fumes coming in the windows from the parking lots. She would keep them shut, but her stuffy apartment needs air to circulate. As always, in the evening after dinner, the blue man streams the blues, closing his eyes and singing the words to "You Put a Spell on Me." But now she's no longer sure what's going to come next. "I might even love you," she whispers to blue man while he sleeps, his hair nesting in the hollow of her rose-colored pillowcase. She says it to the back of his unconscious head, lips dangerously close to his ear, "You're part of my blue period." And then, it's not a dream anymore. One day she wakes up and finds her feelings can be painted blue. When she tells him goodbye, she memorizes the pinkness of his skin under the blue.

The Battle of Silicon Valley at Daybreak

by Alexandria Peary

In a countryside green as a dollar bill,
with the much handled commercial vegetation
from around mall parking lots or in freeway divides,
in a landscape where the wireless has been shut off,
emoji are at war. Emoji are at war
in the mural outside the employee cafeteria
for reading *The Things They Carried* or *Yellow Birds*
or *The Red Badge of Courage:* instead of eating,
emoji are at war.

Outfitted in a list supplied by Wikipedia,
(breastplates, gauntlets, steel collars, mail shirts,
vambrace, pouldron, bassinet, barbute, aventail),
chain armor from a 3-d printer for a smaller budget,
emoji are at war: Blushing Emoji, Frustrated, Weeping,
Smiling Emoji near the village firewall,
& a thousand spears like toothpicks,
emoji are at war.

It's like Where's Waldo. It's like Pac Man.
I spy with my little eye in the "watch-fires of a hundred
circling camps" two generals outside a recharging tent,
a tiny banner unfurling PRIVACY * NET NEUTRALITY
* DEREGULATION. Sound of emoji blood

as the Smiling Emoji advance, swallowing everything,
going postal, kamikaze, road rage, suicide bomber
"hurling down to the House of Death so many sturdy souls,"
sound of emoji blood.

A sword pierces Blushing Emoji #956, Pram's son,
below the groin, and "the dark came whirling down
across his eyes;" a hurled spear is shot through the temple of
Angry Emoji #23, only son of Matthew Thornton
of Boston, and "the dark came swirling thick across his eyes,"
sound of emoji blood. Sound of Emoji blood as Weeping
Emoji #3,418, daughter of the river god, a bullet
plunging into her lung, lodges in the "mortal spot,"
scream fumes.

Outside the village firewall, internet access was slowing
way, way down until the CEO who has her eye on Jim,
a Cubicle Emoji, petitions the Board of Directors
to rescue Jim from his jangling fate of war, seduces him,
gives birth to a daughter ½ Hollywood, ½ New Jersey mortal,
with a weak ankle…Emoji were at war. Whoops,
        the CAPS LOCK IS ON,
so this story ends at the door to the men's restroom.
For we have seen,

I have seen, you have seen, they have seen how emoji blood sounds
like a ringtone of a 50 gun salute in a thousand wavy ploughed
lines, lines, lines, lines where truth is marching on.

The Fig Tree

by Anne Kenner

Because of the virus, we moved to Sonoma, into a little house we have on
the top of a mountain, with its gnarly garden and an ancient, tangled fig
tree whose lower branches are so long and heavy they crushed the post
and rail fence below. When the fence fell, someone, and I don't know who,
propped up the biggest, heaviest limbs on forked branches foraged from
neighboring bay trees. This looks bad-ass.

The fig is ridiculously prolific. Its leaves are lush and massive, and they
unfurl, all together, in the space of a single May week. The tree bears fruit
twice in season. The first fruit, in early July, arrives dainty and purple; you
need to hunt for the figs behind low sheltering leaves or up high inside the
beautiful, snarled arbor. July figs are a little sweet and a little bitter, and
they are gone before you know it.

The late-August fruit, though, is rampant, and it thrives on the tree late
into the fall. These second-harvest figs are huge and brown, ripening in
a matter of hours and bursting open on the branch if you don't pick them
early enough. The birds find the tree first thing in the morning and eat the
shady side of the fruit; when you pick a fig they've visited, you come away
startled by your perfect half.

Fig trees weep when you take their fruit, and the white sap clings and
burns, itches and stings, even after a shower, even if you scrub your skin
with a sponge or a towel or a vegetable brush. You should wear long sleeves
and gloves to pick figs, and carry a sharp pair of shears. But I never do.

This fig is a perfect climbing tree, and I have spent hours in its branches watching the birds forage, reading a book, hiding from guests, or picking fruit that I wasn't meant to find. Our first August on the property, my right foot slipped off a high branch and I fell through the layered branches, through leaves and fruit, toward what should have been the distant hard ground, but ended up, instead, being the perfect cradle of the tree's three lowest branches. My hands were scraped from the grabbing I did on the way down, and my glasses were missing from my head. Otherwise, I felt great.

"This tree," I thought, "just saved me."

Three months later, the tree went dormant. By November, the wide green leaves had shriveled in place; by December their brown husks had fallen to the ground. The few figs at the very top of the tree that neither I nor the birds had managed to grab dangled black and flat against the baring branches. I had never owned a fruit tree before, and had not educated myself about this one. To me, the tree looked deader than dead. I wondered, with all my climbing and picking and tumbling, if it would ever be the same again.

By March, though, the tree was in bud again. When I looked up through the gorgeous skeleton of its arbor, I saw my August glasses dangling from the topmost branch.

The fig comes back bigger, stronger each year, with more fruit than I can handle. I can't harvest it fast enough. Each weekend, I pick buckets to give away at the farmers market, only to find the crop has doubled on the vine by the following Friday. It's a time-lapse thrill, to leave the fruit-stripped tree on a Sunday and return, like Strega Nona, to find it bursting again with fruit five days later. We invite friends and family, we invite people we meet in the grocery store or in a restaurant, to join us for a day of harvest, for our pagan ritual of climbing and picking, itching and scrubbing. It's a paradise when people come; there's enough for everyone. We eat more figs than we save, and we garnish salads and cakes and roasts with the ones that make it into the baskets.

Figs grew along the Nile Valley in ancient Egypt, revered by the pharaohs as trees of life and thresholds to a sacred death. The Israelites shook figs from their trees in Goshen and Succoth, believing the fruit would make them wise. "Figs are restorative," wrote Pliny the Elder, "and the best food that can be taken by those who are brought low by long sickness." Jesus and George Washington considered fig trees righteous. Joan Didion "wanted to be the kind of woman who made figgy puddings." Eudora Welty thought figs "precious and cooling."

I agree with all of these people.

It's a late spring this year, rainy and cold, and the trees and flowers are fighting to bud and bloom. Not the fig tree, though. Twigs are sprouting from every hoary old branch and, from the tip of each shoot, a tiny, three-bladed leaf cups its face to the sky. There are evil conditions in the world, for sure. There is sickness, and those who plan iniquity and covet others' fields. And yet, as Micah promised his benighted neighbors in Moresheth some 3,000 years ago, "Everyone shall sit under his vine and under his fig tree, and no one shall make them afraid."

So there I'll sit.

Thousand

by Katherine Huang

For R.C.

At the market we'd bought a pomegranate,
weighed its cheeks in rubies for luck.
I set my knife to halve it, kneeling in the grass
between red leaves, but you tell me
to let the last hours of the year go in peace –
no sacrifice would convince any god
to stop the season from dying.
With a surgeon's hands, you carve away
the crown, then etch the fruit
into sections that you fan out
over my handkerchief. Second by second,
the arils pebble the pink paisley unbled
while first-grade you-and-I
laugh in the distance, our heads
thrown back on tire swings: backward,
forward-backward, lower, lower-faster.
When the last aril falls, you say
you won't be gone for long
and tread to the horizon, quietly
among these thousand breaths still burning,
where you turn and blow out
a single maple leaf. It hesitates until you
close your mouth, and then, rolling through
the air, goes to join the rest of the sky.

Ode to Pound Cake

by Angie Chatman

The best place to find a tasty slice of pound cake is in the basement of a Black church after Sunday services.

On a typical Sunday, Baptist, AME (African Methodist Episcopal), CME (Christian Methodist Episcopal), and some UCC (United Church of Christ) churches will open their doors at 7am for Sunrise Service, Bible Study at 9am, and the Pastor's Word at 11am.

When I was a girl, our family rarely went to service at a Black church. Instead, we attended Mass at the local parish Catholic church where I went to school. That ritual was about kneeling, sitting down, and Passing the Peace by shaking hands with your neighbors in the pews in front of you, behind you and, if there was enough time, across the aisle from you. During the Passing of the Peace, soft music from a piano or an organ was played. The choir, after Passing the Peace among themselves, sat quietly.

But when my parents attended an event on a Saturday night, my siblings and I stayed over at my grandmother's house and attended services with her the next morning at Bethel AME Church. At Bethel there was also a time during which you Passed the Peace, though it took place earlier in the service, and it was referred to as a Call to Worship. During this segment people walked up and down the aisles greeting old friends and new with handshakes, hugs, pecks on cheeks as if they hadn't seen one another in years instead of the Sunday before.

My grandmother, who was known as Mrs. Conrad at church, was treasurer of the Petite Matrons, a group of women who raised money for community causes sponsored by the church. Everyone knew her. People made their way to our pew to greet her, then they patted our heads or plucked our cheeks, exclaiming how big we had grown, and asked about how well we were doing in school. Although, it was assumed, and rightly so, that we were doing well, as if any of Mrs. Conrad's grandchildren would ever not be doing well in school.

The choir sang two, three, maybe even four songs in the run up to the CME holidays: Christmas, Mother's Day, and Easter. Some people danced in their seat and in the aisles. It was like a celebration until the Pastor rose from his chair and stood at the lectern. My grandmother then handed each of us a piece of Brach's candy, either peppermint or butterscotch flavored, from a pouch in her pocketbook. The choir quieted, and everyone settled down for the Pastor's Word.

Praising the Lord all day like that can make a body hungry, so it was good to know that supper would be provided along with a hunk – the size depends on who's doing the slicing – of pound cake, baked with love by mothers of the church, elders who have "made it through" and therefore, must be treated with respect and deference.

Avoid the pound cake with icing. The only reason a pound cake needs icing is to cover up a flaw. As my grandmother once explained, "A woman needs a basic black dress in her closet, and there's no need to add sparkles and bows to a basic black dress."

If we were patient, we might get another hunk wrapped in plastic and foil to take home for a late-night snack. If we helped to clean up – folding plastic chairs and returning them to the closet or emptying the trash – we could also listen in on grownup conversations and church gossip, which my grandmother called, 'the soap opera of secrets and lies'.

For everything there is a season, and a time for every purpose under heaven… a time to sow and a time to pluck up what has been sown.

Season. From Latin *satio(n-)* a time of sowing

Unlike fruit pies or spiced cakes, chilled puddings or ice cream, pound cake is always in season, on a warm summer day or a chilly afternoon. Pound cake has been in America since its founding, when house slaves or indentured servants did all the sowing in the fields and the cooking in the kitchens, before electric mixers and temperature-controlled ovens. If a household was wealthy enough to own human beings and hire help, then they also had a cow and some chickens out back, in the field, on the plantation.

My grandmother's grandmother was a slave. Her name was Amelia. My grandmother named her oldest girl, my aunt, after her. My grandmother, Ernestine, was named after her father, Ernest, but her middle name was Harriet; she was given that out of respect for Harriet Tubman. A woman who knew that the only way to take care of others was to take care of yourself first.

Until Emancipation, it was illegal to teach a slave to read. Information was passed down via an oral tradition through generations of Black people, via names and memories and stories. Recipes too were narrated – a handful of this, a sprinkle of that, a little more, not so much. Recipes, memories, stories and wisdom are more precious than rubies.

To Season. From Middle English *sesoun* to add flavor

The recipe calls for small amounts of vanilla and lemon juice for aromas of sweetness and tang. Pound cakes were especially popular in the South where to this day "tea" is iced and sweetened unless specified otherwise, and lemon trees thrive in the warm climes. In the early days of pound cake, it is likely that lemon was the only flavor added to those cake batters. The probability is even higher because lemon yellow is the color of pound cake after it's baked.

Vanilla originated in Mexico; it's derived from orchids after pollination; vanilla pods originate from within the flower. A slave discovered how to pollinate the flower by hand, thereby making it profitable to cultivate the pods, though pure vanilla is still very expensive to this day.

The slave's discovery is a reminder: danger comes from within. For this slave also condemned generations of black and brown people to pick yet another fruit for meager wages. Of course, brown and black people picking fruit and vegetables have been and continue to be exploited the world over. Weeping may endure for a night, but joy comes in the morning. Yet what we suffer now is nothing compared to the glory revealed later.

Seasoned. From Old French as *saisonné* ripe, mature, hardened by keeping

The most important ingredient for pound cake is a seasoned pan. By eye and by hand the nicks and cracks are present on the outside. The inside is smooth and supple, honed by years of use by its owner. The cliché, 'don't judge a book by its cover', is exemplified by that pan. People may look hard, beat up, mean, and angry because they are. Be patient and confident in this. God is not through with us yet.

BLACK CHURCH BASEMENT POUND CAKE

1 lb. of butter (all four sticks, softened)

1 lb. sugar (2 cups)

1 lb. eggs (½ dozen)

1 lb. flour (3 ½ cups)

½ cup of heavy cream (do not skimp with a substitution)

1 teaspoon each vanilla extract and lemon juice

The butter and sugar are creamed together until the mixture is a pale yellow, the color of sunshine at dawn. Crack an egg, add to batter, blend, repeat, until all six of the eggs have been used. Next add some of the flour, blend then pour more flour, blend until the pale-yellow color returns at the end of each sequence.

Your arm should maintain a steady rhythm at each stage – crack/blend, then pour/blend – so that it doesn't ache. There's already enough pain in your body from the loves and the losses, the babies and the children, the hurts and the fears, the crying all night, and the dancing 'til dawn.

Add the vanilla and the juice from half a not-too-ripe lemon, blend.

Bake at 350 degrees for about an hour or until it smells good and a knife slid into the middle of the cake comes out clean.

The recipe is deceptively simple. The process of adding and mixing the ingredients is key to a good cake, and a life well lived.

Me, My Father, and The Persian Rug

by Maryam Keramaty

I was at my sister's house and received two phone calls from my father urging me to come right away. My chest was warm with anger. To be pulled away on Christmas Day. Still, I was the only one able to easily get to him. In 2018, this was the kind of rescue mission I had become familiar with, and it was the kind of persistent need from my father that fueled a lifelong strain on our relationship.

"Ok, this will be tricky," I said. I squatted on the wooden floor, worn and exposed, and tugged at the edge of the rug. "We can do this."

My father's wheelchair sucked up the beautiful Persian rug like a vortex. Me, my father, and the Persian rug in an impossible tangle. I directed my father to move backwards by pressing the motorized lever, but I heard only the whir of the motor. I figured the back wheels needed untangling first.

"Dad, go forward, I think I can tug this section out." I tried to pull the rug from the smaller back wheels but the chair was too heavy. My father, the rug, and I were knotted together, ensnarled with no way out.

***

My American mother and my Iranian father fell in love in graduate school in the States and got married. In spring of 1970, they decided to accept my father's San Jose job offer over the offer in Tehran. But that was before they went to sleep. When they woke up, they decided he would take the job in Iran. This decision would affect the family in unknowable ways. It would profoundly impact my identity as an Iranian and build distance in my relationship with my father.

One summer day, in the city bazaar in Shemran, they went to see the rug vendor and bartered over three rounds of tea *chaee*. My father, an experienced businessman, likely negotiated a good deal. I was in my mother's womb as my parents set up a home in an upper-middle class neighborhood and unrolled the beautiful rug. The rug was a showpiece; its colors so rich they seemed to leap off an artist's palette. The blue background, deeper than the ocean blue. Flowered vines in red, yellow, and green. Marked with a golden double border. A nine-by-twelve-foot rug, made from wool threads, knotted by hand, and cut short. Soft to the touch.

***

I remember our backyard in Tehran: fruit trees tended by our gardener, sweet, soft figs in my small fingers, tadpoles swimming in a pool. In a photo, I am in the yard wearing a soft great-grandmother-made-sweater in bright red yarn trimmed in white. I am flushed and bare a toothy smile, on the edge of a giggle. My father is behind the camera. Perhaps I liked the silly thing he said. I know I see warmth and affection between us that day; I see it in my face. Surely, he was a devoted and present father. At least he was then.

***

Childhood memories are clear: the smell of rosewater ice-cream, the sweetness and texture of halvah, the cucumbers from the fruit bowl, driving on winding roads with family to a picnic spot to celebrate the New Year *Noruz*, shopping for pomegranates and persimmons in a bustling bazaar, a chorus of honking cars with no mercy for pedestrians, the warmth from stone-bread *noon e sangak*, sold fresh from the oven. Our patio where we slept under mosquito netting on warm nights and where the rug was shaken out for some fresh air.

***

We were separated from the treasured family rug for over ten years. When the post-revolutionary Iranian government allowed it, the Persian rug, by way of a cargo ship, arrived in Boston Harbor and unrolled again, this time in the living room of our small ranch house in Lexington, Massachusetts. We reunited with the rug, but our lives in America were forever marked by separation and loss.

***

A revolution had been sparked and by December of 1978, millions of Iranians were protesting and demanding the removal of the Shah. Five brown-hued photos in my family album document large student protests: a sea of heads, citizens who want a more progressive Iran. Americans in Iran were feeling unsafe and my mother, sister and I had no choice. Quite hurriedly, we boarded a Pan Am plane to Dulles International Airport in Washington D.C. I always ache to remember we had no time to say goodbye to friends. My father, a production manager who oversaw hundreds of workers in a compressor factory, did not come with us. Perhaps I asked daily for my father. Or maybe adjusting to a new school was enough for an eight-year-old to manage. Either way, the distance between us began to grow.

***

In 1980, my father left Iran and we were reunited in Virginia. We moved into our own home where life was as normal as it could be for our uprooted family. Perhaps my father came to school concerts and teacher conferences, but I don't remember it. I rely on photos to recall this phase of our lives; my father appearing as a strong presence, tall, and capable.

My father had an engineering degree and strived for a better income to support the family, so he decided to go job hunting in Boston. He contracted a virus in the frigid Boston winter. My mother told me later, when I could understand, that the doctors said he might die and they had no idea what was wrong. He was eventually diagnosed with spinal meningitis, paralyzed from the waist down.

At age twelve, I moved with my mother and sister to be near my father in Boston-area hospitals. My mother, sister and I spent most evenings at the hospital and then the rehabilitation hospital. I pushed my father's wheelchair down the hospital hallway. Our family ate dinner in the fenced-in courtyard. We played bingo and won prizes in the rehabilitation hospital dining room.

***

My father made some health gains over the next fifteen years. After the wheelchair, he graduated to a walker, two canes, then only one cane. We stayed in the Boston-area, in Lexington. He opened a travel agency. In rare moments he stood on his own.

***

We managed as a family, but my father's illness was devastating. He no longer fully supported the family financially. His body was severely compromised, but his spirit remained strong and willful. I studied my way through junior high and high school. After college, I moved back home after a job loss. My mother filed for divorce and moved out in 1996. As my father's health declined in his late seventies, his medical needs and concerns overwhelmed the family. He was transported by ambulance when he fell and broke his hip, he felt weakness caused by pneumonia, and suffered another fall and broken leg, to name a few. Things were not going to get better from there.

***

I moved out after ten years of living with my father. My sister and I shared responsibility for his hospitalizations, errands, doctor visits, coordinating home care, and on and on. He was hospitalized again for urinary tract infections, erratic blood pressure, and another broken leg.

I would prepare my father's lunch, and each request was followed by another. The seltzer with ice, a bendy straw, frozen Indian food in the microwave, hot sauce, his special fork, and "Oh, can you make the salad dressing?" With each additional command was that anger, a fiery heat in my chest.

One day, I measured his blood pressure three times and called 911 when he became confused or unresponsive. He refused to go to the hospital. On this day, and many after it, my father made choices that put a burden on me and my sister.

How many times had I urged him to get out of the house? I saw a better life for him, one involving going to a restaurant, a park, the movies. He was most comfortable and secure at home, which I didn't understand, as his only company was pain and loneliness.

Despite it all, I was there by his side, when he had twice left mine.

***

I used pen and paper to process my persistent worry, guilt, and anger, but deep down the ache inside was made of sadness. For losing Iran, its culture, close family ties, stability, and prosperity. For the unfairness of it all. The imposed responsibility my father's paralysis had on me. My anger went unexpressed because it would be cruel to direct it toward a helpless man in a wheelchair. Guilt that I couldn't do more. My father was a burden and I was sucked into his helplessness.

***

The morning after the vortex incident, the rug was removed from the living room. It was folded up under the bed for sixteen months.

***

My father's passing that fall offered relief and sadness. In the spring, my sister and I walked through the family home hunting for relics. Beneath the dust and disarray were treasured reminders of losses we had endured. In the second bedroom, I saw the Persian rug jutting out from under the bed, faded but still magnificent. I told my sister, "I want to keep the rug."

The Diversion

by James Burke

I wasn't supposed to be in Beirut in December 1993. I certainly wasn't supposed to be in a hotel cafe, drinking thick coffee while a dust storm raged outside. I should have been setting up a stall at the Medical Expo in Riyadh for my new employer, Invictus Pharmaceuticals. They wanted to expand beyond the UK and, keen to impress, I had pitched the Middle East as an emerging market. My flight from London had been diverted en route as the storm over Riyadh worsened. We'd landed in Beirut at 1am and after a few hours waiting in the terminal, the airline had finally arranged to put the passengers up in a hotel until our flight could resume.

Exhausted, I slept till two in the afternoon, waking in a panic that I'd missed being called back to the airport. I rushed downstairs, but the concierge told me not to worry, the other passengers were all still there. The storm had moved overnight, and was now covering Lebanon and the surrounding countries. Beirut airport was closed to arrivals and departures. All we could do was wait for it to clear. If I was stuck here more than a couple of days, the whole trip would be an expensive waste and one that was my idea. I was starting to regret overstating all the new deals that would be coming in. Truth was, everything I knew about the expo had come from a guy I'd met a few weeks earlier at a seminar on antidepressants. He'd visited the previous year and told me how great it had been. He hadn't mentioned any sandstorms.

The hotel lobby was grand, but shabby and covered in dust. Every time someone came in a cloud of dirt came in with them. The cafe was next to the lobby, and by the time I'd woken up they'd sold out of everything except coffee. I sat there anyway, waiting for word from the airline, and making notes on my competitors' marketing brochures. Eventually the dust and terrible coffee had driven the other customers back to their rooms. That's where I was headed next when the American walked in.

He was covered in dust and had a red and white checked scarf tied around his face, like a bank robber. Once he'd pushed the doors shut behind him, he beat the dust out of his clothes revealing a blue denim jacket and white jeans. Then he bent over and started to rub his shaggy hair to get the dirt out of that too, changing it from white to blonde. Finally he took off his mask and loudly snorted out of his nose before walking over to the cafe counter to help himself to some water from the jug.

"Can you believe this dust storm?" he said.

I assumed he was talking to the man behind the counter, but when there was no response, I looked up and saw he'd been talking to me. He was tall, and had a thick moustache that looked like it was meant for an older face. He was maybe 30, just a few years older than me.

"Excuse me?" I said.

"Can you believe this storm? They say it's going to last a few days." He took another drink of water.

"Really? I hope not," I said. "I'm flying out as soon as it clears."

"Yeah, that happens. That happens," he said and walked away to talk to the concierge at the check-in desk. I drank some more coffee while I studied my brochures. When I heard a buzzing noise, I looked up and saw him sticking his moccasins under the brush of the automatic shoeshine machine by the elevators. I went back to my work, but after a few minutes he came over.

"Hey, I'm supposed to be meeting someone. You mind if I wait with you?" He sat at my table, and signalled to the counter that he wanted a coffee. "Everyone's always late, it's like island time you know? You here on business?"

"No, I'm not even supposed to be here. I got diverted last night. I'm heading to Riyadh."

"Riyadh? You're better off here! At least here you can get a drink."

"You can drink here?" I said.

"Hell, yeah! Paris of the Med before the war. Big party town."

"I didn't know Muslims drank."

"Sure, they're liberal as hell here. Anyway, the harbor's full of those super yachts. Sailors like their liquor, you know?"

His coffee arrived and he started telling me about Beirut. I knew very little about the place, but he seemed to know everything. He told me about the deal that had ended the war a few years earlier, about how Iranian money was pouring into new building projects, and where you could get a decent steak.

"Are there any restaurants near here?" I asked. "All I've had today is airline peanuts."

"Well, nothing near, but you'd want a taxi in this storm anyhow. I guess you could try…" and then he was listing off streets and neighborhoods that meant nothing to me. I started trying to make notes. "You know what," he said checking his watch, "looks like this guy I'm waiting for has bailed, and there's this bar I've been meaning to try. You want to see the town?"

"Well, that's kind of you, but is it safe out there?"

"Yeah, just wear a scarf. You don't know what's mixed in with this dust."

"No, I mean, aren't there car bombs and… stuff?"

"What? No, no, there hasn't been any of that stuff since, like, last year!"

"Well, I'm supposed to wait here," I said. Going out with a western guide did seem more appealing than being stuck in the hotel.

"Seriously, you're not flying anywhere today," he said, pointing at the apocalyptic scene through the window. "Anyway, when are you going to be in Beirut again?"

He put his scarf back on as we left the hotel, and I pulled my shirt up over my nose, covering my eyes with the other hand. The wind stung as it hit us, and was cold enough that I regretted not bringing a jacket on the trip. It was winter, and I'd been wrong to think it was always hot in the Middle East. There was a taxi waiting just outside and we jumped in. The driver didn't care that he couldn't see more than a few feet in any direction. It seemed like he was using the brake lights in front of him as his guide. He had to drive fast enough to be able to see them all the time, hooting his horn if the car in front slowed down. The sky was orange, and you could only make out silhouettes. At one junction two tanks were parked in the middle of the street, everyone driving round them.

"Is that the army?" I asked.

"Syrians," he said.

We got out of the cab next to a house, surrounded by high rises. The nearest one was covered in bullet marks at ground level, and instead of windows there were blown out holes on every floor. The other buildings looked the same, but then I realized about half of them had open floors because they were under construction. It was hard to tell the destroyed buildings from the new ones in the gloom. He banged on the door of the house, and when it was opened we went into a small bar, full of people.

"I didn't think it would be so busy!" I said. It was a young crowd, and they were playing pop that I almost recognized, but with the words in Arabic.

"Yeah, it's a good night to be out. The secret police can't follow you in a dust storm you know? You can't see them, they can't see you."

"They do that?"

"Yeah, fuck, everyone's following everyone around here. The police, Hez-bollah, the CIA. You know Mossad? They've trained birds to follow people. Fucking birds! Can you believe that?"

We got seats at the bar next to a couple of girls in short skirts, who turned their backs on us as we sat down. We ordered tapas and some watery, local beer that took the taste of sand out of my mouth. The American told me about the Syrian tanks on the streets, and the bombed out buildings. The different religions and factions that shared and divided the city. At one point the power cut out, and the only light was from the candles on the tables. Conversations stopped with a groan, but after a few seconds the music and lights came back on. People cheered and raised their glasses.

"The electric company is broke because everyone steals their power, but people have to steal the power because the company charges too much. It's all corrupt, everyone's on the take. It's nice being able to talk English to someone who doesn't live here. All the other westerners are constantly trying to figure out if they're all bribing the same people, or if you know someone better to pay off. It's exhausting!"

"So how did you end up out here?" I asked.

"I was a ski bum a few years back. I'd travel around, work in countries I wanted to visit, earn some money and then move on. Anyway, I met these Lebanese guys when I was in France and they told me about the ski resorts here. It sounded so nuts I had to see it for myself."

"I had no idea people skied here," I said. I didn't even know that it snowed.

"Yeah, the resorts are pretty decent, about an hour from Beirut. I think the Saudis own them now."

"So wait, you were working in ski resorts during the war?"

"Ha! Well, no. I hadn't done my research. There were no jobs when I turned up so I just ended up skiing and partying and then moved on, but I kept coming back after that. And the war, well, it was a civil war. If you weren't involved it just sort of happened around you. The trick was not getting involved."

"It wasn't dangerous?"

"Well, danger's kind of a rush, and anyway, it's all managed risk. Like, one of the jobs I used to love at the resorts was avalanche control. You go out looking for snow that's starting to build up, and if it is getting to be a problem you drop a few sticks of dynamite and boom!" He smacked his hand on the bar. "That way you set off a tiny avalanche when there's no-one around, rather than a wall of snow hitting your hotel during lunch."

"That's a job? That's crazy," I said

"It sounds crazy, but it's just about knowing what you're doing. About how much risk you're willing to take. It's all about control in the end, like, you sell drugs right?"

"Pharmaceuticals," I said.

"Yeah, so when you develop a drug you do tests on it right? Because you don't want it to work too well. If you cure someone you only get paid once. Better to control someone's symptoms with a drug they have to take for the rest of their life. That's just business."

"That's really not what we do," I said, bristling at the suggestion I sold snake oil.

"Hey, look, I'm not criticizing. You think your drugs work? Good for you. Makes you a better salesman. Point is, most drugs are just avalanche control. You fix the problem today, and wait for it to come back."

I wanted to tell him that was a load of bullshit, but I also didn't want to fall out with him when I wasn't sure how I'd get home on my own. Maybe he was only messing with me.

"So do you go back to America much?" I said, changing the subject.

"No, I don't go back to the States. Once you're on the outside you start to see how it all works. All the rules, all the corporations. Everything's so managed there, the place is like a theme park. You know they put fluoride in the rain there now? In the fucking rain!"

I laughed, but he didn't join in.

"I'm serious, it's in the chemtrails. You see them everywhere now. And then they come over here and start building dams everywhere, you know. Like, they say they're coming here to build hydroelectric dams – the Middle fucking East! Largest oil producing countries in the world? Don't tell me it's hydroelectrics, it's a goddamn weather system. They can make it rain anywhere they want, anytime they want, and they can put any shit in the rain they want."

We were several beers in at this point, and I wasn't sure how serious he was. "We have fluoride in the water in England," I said. "It makes everyone's teeth stronger."

He laughed at that. "Right, like British people care so much about their teeth. It's for population control. It's the same everywhere! It's all part of the same plan. You've got to keep all the different races equal so they keep fighting each other. And the Middle East is a pressure cooker for that shit. You got the Shias and the Sunnis and Israelis and Iranians and you keep building the pressure, and building the pressure and then, bang! Whole fucking place is going to explode!"

"So why stay here?"

"Because this is the only place they can't control, man, the eye of the storm! When everything else breaks apart, this is where they'll rebuild from. Listen, you want some coke?"

"No, I'm… I'm good thanks. I should get back. The airline might be looking for me." I wondered what the penalty was for taking drugs over here. Did they cut your hands off or was that somewhere else?

"Okay, yeah, we can head back soon. I just need to 'see someone'," and he tapped his nose. I thought he'd head for the bathrooms at the back, but instead he went out the front door that we'd come in.

"Is there a phone I can use?" I asked the barman.

He told me there was one out the back so I squeezed my way through the crowd to a corridor behind the bar where some women were waiting for the toilet. I had a number for the airline I could call to get an update on flights, but it was a payphone and I didn't have any local coins. I shouldn't be here I thought. I'd drunk too much and eaten too little, and now I was out with a madman in a city with tanks on the streets. There was an emergency exit next to the phone, so I pushed it and walked out onto the street, wanting to get some fresh air and forgetting that there was a storm outside. The wind slammed the door shut behind me, and there was no handle to open it.

As I started to walk back around the building to the front door, I saw the American leaning into the open window of a black Mercedes, only his white jeans visible. Was that who he was getting his drugs from? He'd talked so much about the secret police I wondered if that was them. Was he setting me up? Jesus, now I was sounding paranoid. I backed away and walked along the street in the other direction, shielding my eyes from the wind. I had no idea where I was going, but maybe I'd be able to find a cab. I looked back to see if they were coming after me, but I could barely see beyond my own arm. At least they can't see me either, I thought, as I headed for the car horns sounding in the distance.

Folklore

by Lindsey Leigh

It is well known that a rock with a hole through it can act as a seeing stone to the other side, but a bone with a hole through it will work even better, giving you the clear and unclouded Sight. Use it wisely.

Weave an effigy with the season's harvest and place it in your home. Bring it food and sing to it softly. When spring arrives, carry it to the field and bury it in the center. If it has felt taken care of, a good harvest is ensured. If neglected, your crops are sure to fail.

Light the tin lantern and observe how the light dances on the wall and the table. Watch it long enough and the streaks of light will form into letters and shapes. It will spell out three things: a secret, a truth, and a portent of things to come.

Hide a shoe underneath your floorboards and the spirit of the wearer will protect your home from evil. Only leave one shoe so the spirit cannot walk off and leave your home unguarded.

Carefully collect fresh morning dew from a spider's web. The dew can be drunk directly or brewed into a tea. After consuming the drink, ley lines will become visible to you, but only at dawn and dusk.

You remember going out to the lake with your friends. You remember waking up in the middle of the night and staring out the cabin window onto the still water. That's when you saw it, beyond the cattails. Your friends asked you if maybe you saw a rock lit by the moon light. But you knew what you saw.

Covid's Metamorphoses

by Katie Hartsock

I know — I know, sorry! Sorry. It's this basement
desk, this heavy rain, that has me thinking of
that wet poem, book one's great flood, the threat made good.

The first bodies to change in Ovid are cosmic,
the sky in love with earth so the horizon is just
a fuck-line, and then men and women and then,

as a crab says to a mermaid in the song my toddler
lately wants on repeat, "Ariel — the human world?
It's a mess." Ergo, a dry decision to start again.

I know the boys are upstairs destroying a train track
they haven't finished building, I know my husband's t-shirt
shows an Imperial AT-AT Walker falling

to its knees at the Battle of Hoth, with *FAIL* in all caps:
the walking tank's last robotic thought, perhaps,
in one of many moments we thought the resistance could win.

And the rain has slowed. When the world is drowning in Ovid,
the waters rise so high dolphins swim through trees,
sleek tips of dorsal fins grazed by the highest limbs.

In their eyes, so much mortality and so much brain,
so well aware of its limits, of what's bearable.

Animal Instinct

by Melissa Mulvihill

We're only halfway through this hike, approaching the longest hill on our walk and Luna's lagging behind a bit. I'm not annoyed. She doesn't like to leave home much and she struggles with serious anxiety. She's nervous today, more than usual. She prefers to avoid people altogether and even though there are frequently people on these trails, she braves herself for me. Also, today there are Cooper's hawks taunting us from above, setting her on edge. They're relentless in their screeches.

We've been good friends going on four years now. She's always ready to be indignant on my behalf. I respect the way she weighs her options between primal reaction and public decorum. Mostly every conversation we have results in the realization that there's more than one way to be a human. She doesn't believe in the perfectibility of the individual. Neither do I. Most importantly, she never mistakes my silence for quiet. Our friendship has grown out of choice, not need. I've never been friends with a dog before.

"Pick a side. You're making me dizzy." I'm polite about it, but I feel like she's herding me.

She's kind of all over the path. First, she's ahead of me on the left with a quick pace that's hard to keep up with. Then she's dragging her feet and falling behind me and to the right. She's glancing around way more than usual as well. I'm not sure she's even paying attention to me.

"Why're you circling around me? I'm trying to talk to you here."

I study the outline of her face in the late afternoon shade. I think that maybe she wants to be listened to rather than listening to me, but that's not it. She's out of sorts today.

She comes to a halt on the hill where new gravel has been recently spread, and both of us slide a bit sideways. The air is crowded and thunder rumbles in the distance.

"Come on. It's getting late," I insist.

She stares at me like I'm something written in a language she doesn't speak and she refuses to move.

"What?" I gesture with expectancy and now some small annoyance.

The Cooper's hawks have silenced themselves.

Her body tenses. She's staring at the ridge in front of us.

The hair on my neck prickles. "Luna, what IS it?"

So far this is a simple story, but true stories are rarely simple.

Right where the gravel hiking trail curves just slightly to the left at the top of the rise, and just to the right of the trail through the trees, beyond the place where shadow flows into sunlight beaming from the low western sun, and perched atop a fallen tree, is a coyote.

My body cycles through all of the physical shorthands for involuntary terror, but I hold my place, aware that I need to convey that I am not distressed prey, here for the easy taking.

Even though my violence is everywhere and my breathing is paused forever, I'm aware of the damp, summer air on every inch of my exposed skin, and the thick stench of mud in my nose from the creek that runs below us. I'm aware that the coyote is about 50 yards away. I'm aware that there is no way we can make it down the path to get help way back in the parking lot if he chases us, or if he decides to call for help. I'm aware of the way the sun drips through the trees and pours around the coyote making his face darker than it should be. I'm aware of the way his white fur lies in contrast to his blonde fur, puffs out in the middle of his chest, and runs up onto his neck and into his muzzle. I'm aware of the way my left hand tightens on my mostly full water bottle.

We all stand here, eyes locked, awareness dawning, options evaluated, and decisions made in this humid moment, the size of just a half of a breath. The coyote's tail flicks slightly. His hackles are raised and so are his hips. He's calling us intruders. He is beautiful only as a warning.

Luna's voice rumbles, her chest a symphony of threat. She is a war cry echoing off the afternoon storm. Her bones and muscles and heart no longer face the right way. Her lips are pulled up and back, her teeth prominent and ready for use. She is shaking from the inside out and she wants to kill the coyote in his skin. She is shredding the air in front of us.

She lunges on her leash, cursing the coyote into the void. A string of obscenities flies from her mouth as she hexes him. She is his calamity and she swears she will tear him to nothing. She is everything and she is imminent.

I wrap her leash around my wrist to hold her near me as gravel flies from under her dedicated paws. The path in front of us ceases to exist for her and she is ripping the heart out of the coyote and stomping it to little pulsing pieces. She fills the forest in front of me, offering her life, guarding my existence.

She is the coyote's last warning, but he doesn't even flinch.

The thunder rumbles low and long, warning that the sky will open soon, dumping its life-giving force here. A vicious crack consumes the forest.

I make myself huge, my survival welling up in my chest, pushing my life up through my throat, across my tongue, and out of my mouth. I am rage. Sometimes the smallest and loveliest places harbor the worst and most useful monsters, the kind that smile at you in the light of day, but will slice you in an instant if darkness descends. My monster roars alongside Luna's and I throw my water bottle with all of the precision I can muster. It lands short of the coyote, but I am surplus evil. I am the shadow side projected onto my enemy. I am a malevolence not fated to end here on this trail with my Luna girl. I maintain eye contact with the coyote, while I shuffle two feet to the left, and pick up the largest piece of wood within my reach. I hold it in the ready position.

The real world is a beautiful mess, governed by unthinking underlying laws and guarded by the deep patterns we trace through the stories we weave as we tumble through our existence. The real world is full of our created meaning, our purposeful mattering, and our becoming. The real world is full of mothers who love so fiercely that when they are driving and they slam on the brakes, their first instinct is to fling an arm out so their children will not crash into glass and go bodily into the night, even though their children are safely strapped in car seats. The world is full of leashed dogs, who love so fiercely that when they are on a hiking trail and a predator presents itself, their first instinct is to act as a shield, flinging themselves in front of their humans, so their humans will not crash into the end and go bodily into the night. It's born into us as genetic information passed down through DNA or not.

I remember somewhere that I read that dominance is about personality and intelligence, rather than brawn, and I wonder which one of us has the best DNA, which one of us has the superior ability to evaluate, and which one of us has a more honed instinct to protect. I wonder exactly which one of us stands to lose more. I wonder if I can safely reach the knife in my pack.

The trees shush about under the orders of the building wind, the underside of the leaves showing themselves, warning us to take shelter. The coyote lowers his head just barely and slightly flattens his ears. His left paw lifts several inches and his tail droops noticeably so it's just lower than his back. I roar again, my voice animal to me, and then I wait.

A few fat raindrops fall onto the trail and thunder rolls across Luna's ferocious growl now vibrating low and resonating in her chest. She's warning that she's not finished. He breaks eye contact, bobs his head low, his tail falling flat against his hind quarters, and he slinks off over the ridge and into the coming storm, never glancing back at us.

We wait several moments, me clutching my big piece of wood and Luna barking with such deep urgency that I barely recognize her voice. Then she's pulling me back down the trail towards the parking lot a mile away. I follow her lead.

We don't speak. We don't stop to see if muskrats are sheltering under the wooden footbridge. We don't pause to hunt for frogs and snakes in the weeds by the pond. We don't slow down to ponder the ancient willow. Every couple of moments she stops to look behind us. She makes eye contact with me every time she circles me counterclockwise, herding me, guarding me, nudging me gently behind my knees. She struts, her tail held high, gloating and snorting every so often with a vicious shake of her head.

When we arrive in the parking lot, I open the sliding door and sit on the edge of the minivan. We're soaked to our skin, but we stop to process what happened. Luna checks me for injury, nudging and licking every part of me, my feet, my knees, my arms. She presses her face into my abdomen, and then licks my neck and face. Only after she is assured that I'm uninjured does she tend to herself.

She releases a cacophony of whines filled with distress and uncertainty, and then she drops at my feet, lying on her back, belly exposed, complaining that enforced proximity via her leash limited her heroism. No, no, no, I sooth. You were brilliant. I drop to my knees right there, in the rain, in the parking lot, the black top radiating a sticky, stenchy heat, and I bury my face in her chest. I tell her that the world is not a theatre for heroism.

I cradle Luna on my lap and whisper to my amygdala, look how close we got, right up to the edge where there is no distinction between things great and small, where all of things that matter stand before us piled up waiting for judgement come due, where everyone is known by standing in relation to the things we protect.

The raindrops sizzle on the pavement, birthing a mist that hovers low over the entirety of West Woods.

I wonder what I am as the strong scent of Luna fills my head, her warnings still slamming off the trunks and the branches and the creeks. Her resolve booms through me. We are shifting in each other's truth, so that when we finally separate, me to drive the minivan, and Luna to resume her place just behind me, I am fiercely unsettled. My fur is drenched and matted from the downpour, my snorts still come at intermittent intervals, my paws ache from the gravel on the trail, my bark is raw from issuing threats, and my claws are sharp, still ready for piercing. My animal instinct refuses to calm, but I will not crash into the end and go bodily into the night.

The Tawny-Green Steppe

by Tim Weed

April 15th, 1832

On the second day of our anchorage at the mouth of the Rio Santa Cruz, I led a party of sailors up to the summit of the hill where I'd stumbled upon an Indian grave. Two large boulders had been rolled up against a cliff, back-filled with rubble, and capped by an immense shard of granite that had somehow been detached from a ledge above the boulders to lie across them like a dolmen. We exerted ourselves to undermine the grave by removing a great deal of the rubble but we found no relics, nor even any bones. It was a disappointment. As the sailors rowed us back out to the ship I was revisited by those feelings of despair, the bleak and nameless melancholy that had dogged me during the first months of the voyage but that had otherwise mostly receded by now, offset by the daily prospect of new curiosities.

The following morning the Captain, myself, and a party of five additional officers and men loaded provisions into the ship's cutter and set off on an upstream exploration of the Rio Santa Cruz. The river was rumored to be navigable all the way to the Andes Cordillera — which I'd yet to lay eyes upon — the great range that curves like a spine from the northern tropics of New Spain to the frigid wastes of Tierra del Fuego.

The trip proved more arduous than we'd been expecting. The Captain divided us into teams and each team took turns ashore, using towropes to drag the reluctant cutter upstream against the current. After a week we'd made disappointingly little progress, though I myself was intermittently distracted by a recurring stratum of sedimentary rock that contained the shells of an ancient ocean.

By the end of the second week the river had dwindled to a rocky stream and the cutter lacked the draft to go on. At first I pressed for us to continue over land, but our stores were nearly depleted, and the Captain was concerned that some unforeseen delay on the downstream journey would put us all at risk of starvation, so I contented myself with a half a day's ascent of the nearest prominence with a westward view, accompanied by the Captain. What a joy it was to gain the crest and see the distant cordillera shining brightly in the mid-morning sun! A line of high peaks running north and south as far as the eye could measure. A parade of monumental cirques and pinnacles capped in pure white like sugar-dusted confections rising up into a crystalline blue sky. To think that in this short lifetime one would have the chance to glimpse such storied beauty with one's own naked eyes.

But in the very next moment the panorama that lay before us — the vast, staggering emptiness of it — turned my mind back to that empty Indian grave. I was gripped by a moment of irrational panic. I shall never see my home again, I thought. I shall surely die out here. My bones will turn to powder and be blown away by this incessant wind.

September 7th, 1832

Resting my elbows on the cathead last night, gazing down into the midnight-black water, I witnessed a remarkable phenomenon. It began as a faint flashing far beneath the surface, like the hint of distant lightning. Gradually the flashes became brighter and more distinct, as if a summer storm were approaching from below.

My exclamations attracted half a dozen sailors and officers of the watch. The quality of the flashing light was eerie, an unearthly bright green whose color I still find difficult to describe. Something like the moon on a clear night but greener; like lightning bugs but quicker to flash and subside. Lightning bugs is the more apt comparison, because as the flashes drew closer each seemed to associate itself with one of dozens of dark cap-sule-bodied creatures weaving quickly through the current a few fathoms beneath the ship.

Suddenly the flashing ceased. I stared down into an ocean so inscrutable it might well have been a great pool of ink. It was as if nothing had hap-pened. As if I and the men leaning over the rail had merely imagined those fast-swimming lanterns under the water. I felt chilled — and surprisingly bereft.

What caused that strange submarine play of lights? I do not know. I suspect that it was fish, or dolphins, or perhaps even a new species of penguin with heretofore unknown luminescent qualities. In the end it is not my ignorance that troubles me, but the feeling that this strange vision is part of something larger that has been hovering on the outskirts of my mind, frustratingly beyond reach of my ability to express in words. The presenti-ment of a devastating truth dwelling just beneath the surface of articulated thought. The dread feeling that there will be no containing it, no reconcil-ing it, no putting it back in its rightful place.

December 23rd, 1832

We sailed into a bay called Wulaia, there to deposit the three Fuegians that had accompanied us from Devonport. I've always considered the captain's plan quite dubious — to set them up as Christian missionaries in their na-tive land — though in truth they were an unremarkable presence for most of the voyage, with days and even weeks passing that I forgot their very existence.

Of the three I knew the young man best: Jemmy Button. Jemmy spoke far better English than the other two, an older couple, and his was the bigger personality aboard the ship. In fact, Jemmy's antic disposition led him to

be adopted by the common sailors as a kind of mascot or jester. He seemed
to enjoy the attention and could be quite the showman; when he said
something that drew laughter he would repeat it over and over, usually
to diminishing returns. Still, he was a jolly young fellow most of the time,
vain of his appearance, always wearing gloves, with his shoes polished to a
flawless shine and his jet-black hair neatly bowl-cut. Before the events of
Wulaia I found the boy sympathetic enough, though it must also be admit-
ted that I considered him slightly untrustworthy — for he was on the one
hand too eager to please, and on the other could never long hold the gaze of
the person addressing him.

On this day, the Fuegians were to be accompanied ashore by their guardian,
the missionary Richard Mathews, whose task it was to oversee the instal-
lation of this advance guard—or Trojan Horse as the case may be charac-
terized—in the conversion of the naked savages of Tierra del Fuego to the
mighty word of God. For a young cleric, Mathews already has too much of
the tight-lipped country vicar about him for my taste. Here at the ends of
the earth, moreover, he strikes me as a creature swimming well out of his
depth. Time will tell, I suppose, but I do fear the worst for him.

The Captain and officers, together with the ship's carpenter and a detach-
ment of sailors, took it upon themselves to build Mathews and his three
charges a hut to live in. This gave me an afternoon at my leisure in the
hills overlooking the bay. I decided to dedicate the time to studying an odd,
orange, spherical fungus that appears to subsist by attacking the branches
of the small-leafed beech trees that cover the land from the waterline to the
snowline. I was keen to discover whether the organism was a parasite or
merely a species of epiphyte, and I wished to examine its internal structure to discover anything else I could about it, including its properties as a
source of nutrition, for Jemmy had assured me that the natives eat it with
abandon.

I followed one of the well-worn Fuegian trails up into the beech forest, pausing in an open meadow to admire the view. Wulaia is more of a protected cove than a bay, with the ship and a scattering of native canoes floating upon the calm, crystalline water that laps the rocky shoreline. Half a dozen breadloaf-shaped islands guard the entrance to the cove, and beyond these the purple-grey channels and endless snowy ranges of Tierra del Fuego. It is an unusually serene vista for this forbidding part of the world. If I hadn't known better I might have imagined the place to be some kind of paradise.

Perhaps Mathews will be successful in his enterprise after all, I fleetingly thought. Jemmy and his cohort will adjust and prosper, and the next English ship to call at Wulaia will find a utopia of Christianized Fuegians dressed in homespun clothes, living in real wooden houses with a small but sturdy chapel of their own construction. It will be a shining example to the rest of the world. A civilized outpost of Empire.

But then the wind picked up, wrinkling the placid surface of the cove far below, and the chill of it caused me to check the buttons of my frock coat. Even as I imagined it I knew that my brief vision of a Christian paradise in these latitudes was unlikely. It's only a matter of time, I fear, before Mathews and his three would-be evangelists are overwhelmed by the hundreds of tangle-haired wretches who haunt this place. Who spend their days out spearfishing in their rudimentary canoes or crouching naked in the bitter cold, filthy and coated with seal fat. Who sleep coiled together like animals in the wet moss. Whose dark glances and shouting, discordant voices bespeak a capacity, I greatly fear, for outbreaks of sudden, brutal violence.

***

I found a colony of the spherical fungus, which grows out of black boles on the twigs and inner branches of the beeches, creating the effect of an oth-erworldly orchard. I made a few sketches, plucked one of the bright orange fruits, dissected it, tasted it. It was moist and extremely bland, with a chewy texture and only a hint of earthy mushroom flavor.

A small greyish bird alighted nearby and I stood observing it bound ener-getically from branch to branch, a tyrant flycatcher of a variety I had yet to collect or identify. Moving very slowly I prepared my net — and with a well-timed flick of the wrist I succeeded in capturing it. The bird put up a determined struggle and when I took it in my hand it trembled and cheeped pitifully. I felt something more than the usual pang of guilt as I reached into the net with my other hand to take its little head in my fingers and snap its neck.

This done, I gathered up my instruments and strode down through the beech forest to the shore of the cove, humming a little tune as I went in an unsuccessful attempt to lighten my mood.

The hut was already built, a solid-looking cabin made of stripped beech logs. Save for my own jollyboat the landing craft had already returned to the ship, and Mathews and the older native couple sat on the stoop of their new home, looking ill at ease as a mob of perhaps two dozen naked Fue-gians importuned them. The rowdy chatter of the mob was underlined by the piercing shouts of the three men closest to the hut, who gestured with their fishing spears in a way that seemed to communicate escalating hostil-ity. For a moment I thought it might be up to me to rescue these recently settled shipmates — I caught Mathews' eye and held up my fowling piece with an inquiring look — but the young missionary, though pale and tight-lipped with fear, waved me off.

It was with a measure of relief that I strode along the cobble shoreline to where I had beached the jollyboat, only to find Jemmy, crouched beside the vessel in an apparent attempt to conceal himself from the wrath of his clamoring countrymen.

"Good day, Mr. Darwin," the boy said. "I shall return to the ship with you please."

"Now, now, Jemmy," I said, overturning the boat and dragging it down to the tideline. "This place is your true home. Aren't you happy to be back?"

"I wish to return to the ship."

"Well, my boy," I said, busying myself with affixing the oars. "I do understand your feelings, but unfortunately that's not the arrangement you made with Mr. Mathews, and it's not really my place to intervene. Why don't you go back and sit with the others? You may be surprised. I'll wager some of these people will remember you if you tell them you were born here."

"Please, Mr. Darwin." The boy, clearly close to panic, waved a hand in the direction of the increasingly angry natives crowding the front of the hut. For a moment I considered letting him climb into the jollyboat, but that would have been directly contrary to Mr. Mathews' wishes, and, by extension, the captain's too.

"I'm afraid you're going to have to stay on, Jemmy, at least for now. I'll discuss it with the Captain tonight, and we'll send word of his decision in the morning before we sail. What do you say?"

The young Fuegian threw himself to his knees on the far side of the boat with both hands clapped tight to the gunwale. His whole body trembled — putting me in mind of the little flycatcher — and his wide-set eyes brimmed with tears of despair. "Morning will be too late, Mr. Darwin."

"Don't be silly. Go sit beside Mr. Mathews and the others on the stoop or hide yourself within the hut. Everything will quiet down soon enough, you'll see."

"These people will take God away from me. They have promised as much."

"Take God away, Jemmy? Don't be ridiculous. God is everywhere and belongs to everyone. He lives inside your soul. No one can 'take Him away'."

"You think you understand, but you don't." The boy's voice had acquired a hard edge, and I felt myself losing patience. I finished mounting the oars and tried to pull the nose of the boat down over the last of the cobbles and into the crystalline wavelets, but it wouldn't budge.

"I must get back to the ship now, Jemmy. Remove your hands or I shall be forced to remove them myself."

Jemmy sighed and got to his feet. "You will have me go to Satan then, Mr. Darwin?"

"You mustn't take Mr. Mathews' teachings quite so literally, Jemmy. You do understand that Satan is just a metaphor, don't you?"

"And what about the soul, Mr. Darwin? Is that a metaphor too?"

"No, Jemmy. Satan is a metaphor, but the soul is real."

"Are you sure about that, Mr. Darwin?"

"Quite sure, Jemmy." I turned away to finish dragging the jollyboat down into the water, and when I turned to give the young Fuegian a final word of encouragement he had melted into the beech forest. Shrugging, I pushed off and leapt into the boat.

Halfway across the glassy cove to the ship, I spotted Jemmy standing stark naked in the shadows at the edge of the trees, his English clothes pooled darkly on the cobbles beside his newly bared feet. I shipped the oars and took up my spyglass to focus in on the young man's face. It gave me a shudder — though I'm not sure why I was surprised — to discover through the magnified lens that he was staring straight back at me.

And it was odd. His eyes had lost all trace of fear.

March 13th, 1833

We have sailed north to the mouth of the Rio Negro. The captain feels compelled to redo his survey of the coast, collecting additional data points to provide the Admiralty with the most accurate detail possible. It is an exacting, time-consuming process, meaning that I now have a blessed three weeks free to dedicate to naturalizing before I am required to rejoin the voyage at Bahía Blanca.

In a crumbling cliff near the river mouth I discovered a number of fossilized bones from a large extinct mammal. On the following day, embedded in porous limestone, I found an immense skull that I first thought might pertain to an ally of the rhinoceros. However, a closer study of the jaw and several intact teeth thrillingly revealed that I am in possession of the remains of a Megatherium, or perhaps even a Megalonyx — the only previously discovered specimen of which is locked away in King Ferdinand's collection in Madrid.

Once these invaluable fossils were safely crated up and made ready to send back to England, euphoric from my discoveries, I set out on a horseback expedition under the protection of half a dozen gauchos who are acting as scouts for the Argentine Confederation's ongoing campaign against the Mapuche Indians. On the first day we rode west into a spectacular open steppe, a vast expanse of wild grassland teeming with guanaco, a russet camelid, and rhea, a great flightless bird like an ostrich that flees before our horses on long, dainty legs. The gauchos showed me how they use their bolas to bring the giant land birds down.

I could not accomplish anything with a bola other than to provoke a round of boisterous laughter when I managed to entangle the legs of my own horse. But I did manage to shoot one of the birds, which I skinned and cured and packed in a saddlebag to add to my growing collection.

March 17th, 1833

The gauchos are extraordinary. They seem to have fitted themselves to the landscape in much the same way as the guanaco and the rhea, with a natural seat that seems to transform horse and rider into a single creature unified in body and mind. Noticing me watching them, the men spur one another to ever more daring feats of horsemanship, such as letting go of the reins to lie back on the saddle with their feet crossed comfortably on the horse's neck, or slipping out of the saddle altogether to stand motionless on one stirrup as if borne through the air beside the galloping horse.

The leader of the scouting party is a military captain named González. He is three years my senior, the son of a wealthy rancher, sharp-eyed and rugged, a crack shot with his well-used Brown Bess musket. It's obvious that he's earned the trust and respect of all his men, and he possesses the most remarkable cat-like grace, a comfort within his own skin the likes of which I've observed — in human beings at least — only once or twice before. It's a wonder to me. An inspiration.

I find myself emulating the Argentine's mannerisms and saddle posture. I've traded my extra pair of riding boots for a gaucho outfit of my own, complete with a woolen poncho and cotton bombachas and a scarlet kerchief, which I wear knotted loosely around my neck, just like the capitán.

March 24th, 1833

After ten days of horse-borne travel across the pampas, I find myself taking on the ways of a gaucho to a surprising extent. I sip my gourd of yerba maté in the mornings and smoke a cigar at any hour. When the day is done I lie with my poncho as my only covering, with the southern hemisphere stars as my canopy. And what stars! A vast expanse of pinpoints more vivid than any night sky I've heretofore witnessed. Millions of spark-bright diamonds strewn across the velvet universe in a fit of crazed exuberance. A textured, multi-layered field of constellations so vivid and unfamiliar it's as if I've been reborn into an entirely new world. Sometimes, as I stare up at them, I feel as if my spirit is merging with those of every living being that has ever existed or ever will exist. My mind reels with an ecstatic intuition of destiny.

And in the next moment this will all melt away, leaving me bereft and disconsolate once again. I'm beginning to suspect that my Christian faith has always been weak. Since childhood, for example, I've harbored a secret suspicion that life has no meaning after all. That the human soul, contrary to the words I spoke so confidently to Jemmy at the end of our acquaintance, is nothing more than a fleeting and illusory construct. A fiction we create—a metaphor—to keep ourselves from having to face up to the great emptiness of the universe.

Naturalizing has been a way of keeping that suspicion at bay. The study of creation in all its complexity and wonder has served as a reassuring reminder that there is indeed some kind of ordering intelligence out there. There are times, though, when I feel as if I am not looking up at the sky at all, but peering downward into a vast abyss.

March 29th, 1833

At dawn I awoke to find the rest of the party gone save for González, who rested on his haunches beside my sleeping place smoking a cigar and gazing pensively down at me. The others were on a reconnoitering mission, he explained, and would be back before nightfall.

"We're staying put all day, then?"

"Yes, my friend. You are free to attack the rocks with your little hammer, or to shoot a few of our harmless birds." Grinning, González filled a maté gourd with steaming water from a pot by the fire and held it out to me. I sat up and took it gratefully, feeling a stirring of excitement: we'd been crossing miles and miles of tawny-green steppe every day without cease, passing many an interesting rock formation or well-vegetated gully that I would dearly have liked to explore.

I set off on my own. I made some interesting finds, too, including two new species of beetle, an Indian arrowhead, and an elegant bryophyte, the tiny yellow leaves of which I sketched out carefully in my journal in case the process of drying and preserving them should alter their fine antler-like structure.

I came back to camp just as the gauchos were riding in, dust-covered and spent-looking. I perceived something new in their demeanor, a kind of shared secrecy about their recent activities, that made me slightly uncomfortable. It was an odd reaction, and for the moment I couldn't pin it to anything concrete. It was as if a day apart, absorbed in our own pursuits, had imposed a distance between these men and myself that hadn't existed before. I hadn't realized the extent to which I'd been enjoying the feeling of camaraderie among this party of scouts, and the distinction of being considered an honorary member of the expedition.

When one of the men called out my name, I therefore looked up eagerly from my sketching. The gaucho who'd spoken stood beside his horse, with González standing beside him, gazing down at me with broad, expectant grins.

"Good news, Mr. Darwin," González said, lightly patting the gaucho's saddlebag. "This man has brought a specimen for your collection."

I hurried over, eager to see what strange species the gaucho had found for me on the pampas. I hoped it wasn't something I'd already observed. Perhaps it was an exemplar of that elusive rodent, the tuco-tuco?

The gaucho grinned, resting his hand protectively on the buckle of his saddlebag as if relishing my suspense.

"*Vaya, muchacho,*" González said, nodding to the man. "Go ahead and show him."

The gaucho lifted the stained leather flap of the saddlebag and reached in to withdraw the cloth bundle containing the specimen, which he unwrapped and held up for my inspection. It was mammalian, dark and round-bodied, its long fur blackened by gouts of coagulated blood. I leaned in to get a better look, then let out a yelp of dismay and staggered backward, tripping over a tussock to pitch belly-up in the pampas grass.

The men responded with a cascade of uproarious laughter. I felt myself coloring deeply, even through the horror.

The specimen was a severed human head. I could see from the square shape and prominent cheekbones of the face beneath the streaks of dried blood that it belonged to a South American Indian, likely from the Mapuche tribe, the war against which forms the rationale of the scouting expedition I have until now been so heedlessly enjoying.

The gaucho held the head by its hair and shook it at me where I lay, letting out an exaggerated moan. He was rewarded by another outbreak of hearty laughter from the men.

"What's troubling you, Mr. Darwin?" González asked, a mirthful smile playing at the edges of his mouth. "Do you not like your new specimen?"

I was unable to answer. Feeling a sudden irresistible pressure in the bottom of my esophagus, I turned to empty the contents of my gut into the grass.

It was the eyes I couldn't get out of my mind. Wide-open as if permanently surprised, yet as devoid of expression as a pair of dirt-flecked hard-boiled eggs.

"Come now, Mr. Darwin. Are you really so delicate? You are aware that these people have no souls, aren't you?"

I sat up, wishing more than I've ever wished for anything to erase the image from my mind.

But I could not erase it. And I could not unsee it.

Can Your House Kill You?

by Amber Wong

I squeezed past Maya and closed my office door behind her, shutting out the last rays of natural light. Under the cool fluorescents, she was already at work, reaching past her rounded belly to sort documents on the table, preparing to brief me, her new manager, on the results of the recently finalized 1996 Palermo Wellfield site investigation. When her dark hair cascaded forward and she brusquely tossed it back, I hid a smile. We were rarities, Asian American women engineers infiltrating a white-male-dominated field, constantly challenged to prove that we belonged. To fight back, we assumed gestures of no-nonsense professionalism. She reminded me of my younger self.

I'd worked at the US Environmental Protection Agency for eleven years, mostly in water programs, and was thrilled with my new management role in the Superfund cleanup program. Over the past month I'd been poring through the underlying law and enabling regulations while acquainting myself with my staff and their responsibilities. The Superfund law, the 1980 Comprehensive Environmental Response, Compensation, and Liability Act, was complex and powerful. Enacted in response to the disastrous public health crisis at Love Canal, it gave the Superfund program a clear mandate: discover, and clean up, the worst of the worst hazardous waste sites in America. Polluters would pay for cleanup. One sledgehammer provision – and one of the most controversial – was that where there were multiple polluters of a site, even small contributors could be liable for the entire cleanup. Finally, if no viable responsible parties could be found, the government would pay.

Maya was a site assessment manager, part of a gatekeeping team working to identify sites bad enough to be put on the National Priorities List, known colloquially as the Superfund list. She'd already overseen the sampling work, already roughed out a hazard score using EPA's national formula. After this meeting, she and I would make a recommendation to our top management about whether the site warranted a Superfund designation. Most sites didn't make it this far. But when a site hit the high bar of "imminent threat to public health and the environment," EPA would solicit public comment prior to Superfund listing. Once listed, those high priority sites were turned over to remedial project managers for cleanup. In the past, hard data and good science drove listing decisions, but in the super-charged political environment of 1996, the site assessment program had hit an inflection point. States could now block Superfund listing. Claiming that Superfund put an unnecessary stigma on property, most states refused listing of any new site. Maya was here to brief me on the gravity of the environmental problem and the severity of the political pushback.

She slid the Palermo Wellfield Site Inspection report across my office table and scooted her chair next to me. "Ready?" she asked, her dark eyes alert for my reaction. Although I might have been projecting, I sensed a bit of her unease. How well did I understand the site assessment program? How much detail did I need? She probably knew that, like her, I was a civil engineer. She might have heard that I'd had six years of engineering experience in private industry prior to my eleven at EPA, and that I was known in the agency for my technical chops.

Maya opened the site inspection report and flipped to the summary page. "Our contractors did a good job, they chose the right sample locations," she began. "The data clearly show there's a real problem." Thick with sampling data and maps, the site inspection report laid out the dry facts of our case. Like every great detective, because every site investigation is a detective story, Maya worked backwards from "dead body" to "possible suspects." First, the metaphorical body. Routine sampling by the City of Tumwater had caught dangerous concentrations of trichloroethylene (TCE) and per-chloroethylene (PCE), known carcinogens, in the City's tap water. Levels exceeded safe drinking water standards. In addition to health risks from ingestion, tap water sprayed from household faucets and shower heads could vaporize. Tumwater residents were at risk both from drinking the water and inhaling the solvents.

To their credit, the City took quick action, switching to a clean water supply while they searched for the cause. Samples taken at the wellfield — the source water — also showed high TCE, indicating that the aquifer was contaminated too. Where were the solvents coming from? The aquifer, like a slow underground river, had to be carrying the contaminants from an upstream, or upgradient source. Searching for possible users of TCE or PCE in the area, the investigation turned up two possible sources: a Department of Transportation site which could use TCE to clean equipment, and a dry cleaning shop which could use PCE in its cleaning process. No smoking gun had been found, but all we needed to move forward was probable cause.

Maya smoothed out a well-worn location map in front of me. "Let's look at the direction of groundwater flow," she said. As I gave the map a quick once-over, I almost gasped as my finger underscored a telling detail: the map title.

I turned to Maya with a wry smile. "So, wait a minute, this Palermo wellfield is in Tumwater, Washington?" She nodded briskly, and I warily shook my head. Still smiling, I asked, "So just for reference, where's the Olympia brewery?"

Olympia beer commercials, then pervasive in the Pacific Northwest, touted the natural artesian water of Tumwater, Washington as their secret ingredient. One jingle even ended with the slogan, "It's the water, and a lot more." With damning data about the Palermo aquifer right in front of us, and the sure knowledge that pollutants can spread, the catchphrase felt badly misplaced, if not a bit sinister.

Maya's brows shot up as she stood to scan the map. She knew exactly what I was thinking: *Does the brewery pull from that aquifer?* At last she pointed to the edge of the map and rubbed her forehead in relief.

"No, no, the brewery's upgradient. Not affected at all. Oh, and besides, they don't brew with well water anymore, they're hooked up to the City water supply now." When my eyes widened in alarm, she quickly clarified, "The City of Olympia, not Tumwater!"

We laughed together, in mutual respect. An EPA public relations disaster had been averted, although the Olympia brewery and their advertising agency had some explaining to do.

She swept back her dark hair and leaned over the table. Tapping first on the dry cleaner site and then the Department of Transportation site, she drew her finger toward a web of roads that marked a residential neighborhood. "There's the Southgate Dry Cleaner, the big source of the PCE, and the DOT site, the source of the TCE. Here at the bottom of a steep bluff is the Palermo neighborhood. The site scores because the Palermo Wellfields over here — the target," she met my eyes, checking for understanding, "provide drinking water for the City of Tumwater. There's a direct human health risk. Just being over drinking water MCLs — maximum contaminant levels — is enough to score."

I lapsed into engineering shorthand. "So we need to air-strip the wells?" Air stripping, a common treatment, was part of my graduate school curriculum and private sector experience.

She looked impressed but apologetic. I'd identified the likely technical solution, but we weren't there yet. "No, not *us*," she patiently explained, waving her hand between us. "The site assessment program determines if the site qualifies as a Superfund site, and later, after it's listed, the *remedial* program figures out the remedy. We need to list it first. Here's what we know. We know the site scores because drinking water is affected." She turned back to the map. "But there's another big problem." From pictures on my desk, she must have known I was a single mom, and in her frown I saw the deep concern of the young mother she was soon to be. She pointed to the bottom of the bluff, and her voice rose with new urgency. "See these backyards? Water pools up there when it rains! Is it groundwater or storm water? Is it contaminated? When we were out there drilling sampling wells, we saw lots of kids playing in their yards!" I grimaced and started to respond but caught myself as her voice dropped ominously. "And that's not all."

My chest tightened. *Not all?* People were drinking carcinogens, kids might be splashing in carcinogens. The danger wasn't just hypothetical. How could it be worse?

She waved her hand over the map of the whole neighborhood. "Look, that groundwater flows *under* their houses. If some TCE or PCE vaporizes, it can seep up through the soil into their crawl spaces and into their homes. So there's the potential for vapor intrusion, like with radon gas. While they're at home, they could be breathing it too."

Oof. I sat stunned, virtually gut punched. Pollution could stalk you, creep into your house, get that personal. Vapor intrusion is such an insidious threat. Everybody breathes. Unlike dealing with tainted drinking water, you can't just buy bottled air.

How would you clean that up? The air, the water, the soil? Although Maya had gently reminded me that we weren't at that stage yet, my engineering brain was already racing ahead, sorting facts, spotting data gaps, and riffling through options. This site hit the jackpot, the trifecta of Superfund exposure pathways: direct contact, ingestion, and inhalation, or more simply, touching, drinking, and breathing. Direct contact and ingestion were complicated, but the Superfund program had done this many times. We knew the science, knew how to calculate the risk, knew how to clean it up. But how do you even begin to evaluate the risk of the inhalation pathway to Palermo residents? You'd need to know how much TCE and PCE is inhaled, and how dangerous it was. Like a Rubik's cube, there were so many interlocking variables. Adults have larger lung capacities than children, but children might be more vulnerable. Other sources of solvents in the home – off-gassing from formaldehyde insulation or household cleaning chemicals – might add to, or even overwhelm, the groundwater contribution. Cracks in a floor slab could increase the amount of vapor intrusion, but people who left their windows open would have less. Levels of TCE and PCE in each home could vary depending on the house's location in the neighborhood and individual family habits. Were they close to the bluff? Did the residents leave their windows open in the winter? In the summer? What household cleaners did they store under the sink? As regulators, our challenge was huge. We needed to answer any resident's bottom line question: *Is my home safe?*

"So what do you think?" Maya's measured voice brought me back to the decision at hand, step one in a well-defined process. "The site automatically scores because the risk to drinking water affects the people of Tumwater." She sat down beside me, notebook open, pen poised.

It seemed like a slam dunk, but had I missed something? Earlier I'd been warned that not every site that scored should be put on the Superfund list. I tried to read her face and buy some time. "And the air problem?"

"We don't need air to score the site. Drinking water's enough."

In that moment I thought of my elementary-school-aged sons, how they drank from our tap and ran in our yard. How they sat in their rooms to study or to play with their friends. Like any other kid, they were oblivious to any environmental danger and simply assumed that home was safe. And that I, their mom, would keep them safe.

I focused on Maya's eyes. "What's your recommendation?"

She settled back into her seat and absently folded her hands over her swollen belly. Her dark eyes held an intense look of absolute certainty. "If the remedial program does it right and puts in the air strippers, they'll fix the water and air problems at the same time. If the state of Washington agrees, I recommend we move the site forward for listing."

Much to our surprise, citing the imminent threat to Tumwater's drinking water supply, the state agreed to make Palermo a Superfund site. The site was listed in 1997. Within a year — in one of the fastest cleanups on record — a soil/vapor extractor was pulling PCE out of the soil at the dry-cleaner site. A year later, two air stripping towers were actively purging the drinking water wellfield of solvents. A subdrain was installed at the bottom of the bluff to intercept contaminated groundwater before it surfaced in neighborhood yards. These quick actions were aimed at breaking both the ingestion and direct contact pathways.

The inhalation pathway proved more difficult. EPA promised to investigate the groundwater table throughout the entire neighborhood and recommend fixes if needed.

Construction was complete on January 30, 2001. All that was left was to monitor the site to ensure the remedy was working properly. We applauded a major milestone, and I left the Superfund program in May 2002.

***

Close to 20 years later, I've since retired from the EPA, Maya's son is out of college, and the Palermo Wellfield project is still active. Is the site safe? Is the remedy protective? Not according to a terse statement in the latest Five-Year-Review, completed in 2018, which cites unsafe levels of TCE vapors from groundwater in at least one house, and determines that the subdrain at the bottom of the bluff isn't intercepting groundwater as well as expected. Superfund's Five-Year-Review exists for exactly this purpose — to check whether the remedy's protective and beef it up if it's not.

The review process also allows EPA to update the remedy to include advances in toxicological research. In 2011, when TCE exposure in pregnant women was found to increase the risk for fetal heart defects, EPA's quest to find, measure, and remediate vapor intrusion in the neighborhood reached a fever pitch.

"I knocked on every door in the neighborhood, pleading with them to let us sample their air," says EPA's current remedial project manager, a friend of mine – and a mom – when I reach her over the phone. "Everyone, especially prospective parents, needed to know the dangers were real. I brought our hydrologists and toxicologists, and we answered their questions until late at night. We tried so hard to win their trust. Finally, about 30 of the 47 households at one point said yes." She pauses, then lightly adds, "Meanwhile, our technical staff was scrambling to determine the best way to sample those homes."

Turns out, it wasn't easy to get meaningful data. It was hard to nail down the ghoul in the room, the unseen, odorless, airborne toxin that might or might not exist. Other cleaning supplies in their homes, like Lysol and bleach, interfered with TCE measurements. Dry-cleaned clothing was a problem; a wedding dress that had been preserved 20 years prior was still off-gassing. Heavy rain even affected vapor intrusion levels.

But they did it. Now, armed with a working sampling protocol — and a science-based not-to-exceed action level — EPA can keep Palermo residents better informed of the risks.

"If you measure concentrations above the 2 microgram-per-cubic-meter action level, what can you do?" I brace myself for a multi-million-dollar treatment solution — the kind that the Superfund program is always vilified for.

Her high-pitched laugh throws me for a loop. "The fix is easy! It's the same as for radon. Google 'radon mitigation.' Lots of radon companies can install a home venting system for under a couple thousand dollars." I'm astonished that the technical solution's so simple, but my hopes are dashed when she continues, "But the house with the acutely high concentration? The DOT offered to install a venting system for free, but the residents refused. We keep trying to reach them, but they won't respond."

Why are they in denial? Like residents at other Superfund sites I've dealt with, not everyone wants to know they have a problem. Why would you still live in a house that can kill you?

Her voice grows louder, and I sense her frustration. "Vapor intrusion's such a crazy pathway. The science, the sampling protocol, the action level — nationally, Palermo's on the cutting edge, and we're confident about what we can do when we pinpoint a problem. More data could help us find those houses, but…"

As she lapses into silence, a verbal shrug, I feel for her. It's the scourged blessing of Superfund: the power and urgency to act, pitted against the time needed to gather conclusive evidence to justify that act. On one hand, our project managers must select cleanup remedies that protect people and the environment. On the other, those remedies can't be too expensive or place an undue economic burden on the community. At Palermo there's even another hurdle. Because the remedy must be placed in residents' homes, we need to secure their permission. Contrast that to Love Canal, the famed "first of the worst" site, where the health danger was so obvious and extreme that shortcuts were justified. Residents were simply evacuated. But most sites don't warrant such quick and costly — not to mention disruptive — solutions.

She sighs, muted now. "It really comes back down to the personal. Does the community trust us? They're scared. We're dealing with real people here." I'm just about to say it, but she beats me to it when she blurts, "Their health is all that matters."

Letter to the Future

by Mee Ok Icaro

Soojin texted bright and early, hoping to gather Alexis and me for prep. It was time for our close-up: two international adoptees back in the motherland making our debut on national television. The Korean CNN — YTN — the country's first all-news TV channel, would be taking us to *Bugak Palgakjeong* Pavilion, one of the highest peaks in Seoul, offering sweeping panoramic views of the city. Unlike the famous *Namsan* Seoul Tower with its teddy bear museum, children's theater, food court, restaurant, digital high-powered telescope, cable car or dramatic "light art" calling attention to itself after sunset, *Bugak Palgakjeong* Pavilion remains free of tourists. No wishing pond. Nothing to give it the reputation of being a romantic mecca, nothing to lure movie stars to secure their padlocks on the roof deck fence to symbolize their eternal love, and throw away the key. The pavilion is a quiet affair, a place better suited for older couples than young lovers — or those who wish to remember those no longer with us.

When the YTN van pulled up, out stepped two cameramen who spoke no English and a young, beautiful producer with the best English I had yet heard spoken by a native Korean. On the way, I would learn that she had spent a year in New York City as an English major studying Jane Austen.

"Hello, I'm Junghwa." She bowed deeply. "Thank you so much for doing this."

Soojin initiated a short exchange with her and the cameramen to make sure our interview stayed on the rails, before we all piled into the van to begin our drive across town toward the Blue House — Korea's White House — and beyond.

Our ascent up *Bugak* Skyway involved driving through a 19-mile forested village peppered with the residences of Korea's elites: politicians, celebrities, and industry titans. As we drove up the dizzying mountain, the landscape grew lusher and more canopied, hiding us in its nestled wilderness. Then, suddenly, a flash of golden light would interrupt the shadowy vegetation, breaks in its ancient forests revealing a "Hallyu" starlet's avant-garde abode or a taste of the promised view of Seoul from the top, as the city receded farther and farther into the distance.

Once at the summit, we climbed the stairs of the octagonal pagoda to a scenic spot where all of Seoul would serve as our backdrop. But after the suspense of our drive, seeing it in its completeness from such a great height felt like a lie. From here its streets were muted and the buildings felt empty. With enough distance, all cities seem still. I pretended to snap photos on my phone as they filmed me taking in the vast space between *Bibong* and *Munsubong* Peaks, a valley flooded by a brief stint of civilization, and bookended by the eternity of its commanding mountains. No wonder it was once where Korea's ancient kings built stone walls to guard their palaces from Chinese and Manchurian invaders.

As the cameras rolled, I tried to imagine what all of this looked like when I was born but before I was adopted, when it was still recovering from being the most decimated major city in the history of the modern world after the armistice was signed between the US and North Korea in 1953. Staring at the other mountains towering over the cityscape, I wondered how many secrets they held.

Junghwa and I walked along dappled paths, pretending to be steeped in conversation, collecting footage and beauty. After Alexis was filmed, peeking through the tower binoculars that overlooked the city and showing childhood photos to a charmed and captivated Junghwa, we were shown an oversized red mailbox called "Slow Mail," a place where people post letters to be mailed in a year's time, like an epistolary time capsule, a letter to the future.

An extension of the "Slow City" movement headquartered in Italy, the first Slow Mailbox in Korea was installed in 2009 as a breath-catching reaction to the fast-paced delirium of one of the world's most modern cities and had since spread throughout the country. They come in many shapes and sizes, but are always handsomely painted — usually fire-engine red — with either Korean characters or simply the word "Post." This one was the biggest in all of Korea, the size of a small telephone booth. Standing in front of it made one feel small, like a child, when most of the world was unreachable.

Junghwa handed us stationery from the gift shop, cards with a watercolor painting of a house surrounded by flowers instead of a fence, and led us to separate picnic tables where we penned messages to our faceless birth mothers who would never see them. After being filmed under the shade of the spruce trees as we wrote with bowed heads, we took turns reading our letters to the camera. I went first. My message was warm but prosaic; I had said everything in the letter I had written to the mysterious woman who birthed me before I arrived. I had already screamed into the void and sliced those veins — and the blood had already dried.

But Alexis had not yet gone there. She began reading as she might any piece of writing — a deep breath, a touch of nerves, and a clumsiness of a voice trying to find its rhythm as the lens of the cameraman stared at her. "Dear Mum," she began in her sometimes British, sometimes Danish, sometimes Spanish accent. "I don't know if you'll ever read this, but I wanted you to know that I'm here in Korea… lookin' for you." She paused. "I know we've never met, but if you could see me — " she stopped, staring down at the piece of paper shaking in her hands.

Junghwa and Soojin glanced at each other. "I'm sorry," Alexis apologized.

Then she continued.

She began to describe how, when she was a child, she would think about her birth mother, wonder what she looked like and how she was. She read on until she couldn't, until she melted into inconsolable tears, a grieving star collapsing under the profound weight of its own unclaimed existence, until she sat holding her letter, palms open to the sky, like an empty offering.

The cameramen quietly lowered their cameras. Soojin sat at her side, and asked if she would like to stop. Without looking up, Alexis confessed, "I can't keep readin' this."

Once she calmed down, we heard Junghwa's voice gently explain, "There is one last shot. It doesn't require any talking. Would you feel comfortable doing that?" We were to walk across the landing with our letters and place them in the Slow Mailbox, with all of Seoul and its mountains as our witnesses.

"Yeah, okay. I just need a minute," Alexis began wiping her eyes. "You're smart, Mee-ok," she looked up at me. "You brought sunglasses."

After she gathered herself we waited for the cue, then tried to casually walk to the massive mailbox. But when we went to open the slot, it wouldn't budge. We turned and stared helplessly into the camera. Soojin came running over, her dress straight out of a magazine from the 1940s — a long, flowing, flowery skirt and perfect Korean hair billowing behind her. She tugged at the handle, then called out to Junghwa in Korean.

It was locked. Slow Mail wouldn't be taking any letters that day.

Exposure

by Nick Zelle

When I asked you to take off
        your neon orange trucker hat
to sit for a photo between two trees,
        I did feel embarrassed for you,

awkward to have tasked myself
        with slightly undressing a friend.
I could tell by your open mouth
        that you were genuinely distracted,

awaiting the first shot. Your sundress
        pooled around your knees in the grass,
and you poked at ants.
        It didn't suit you,

posing, or being posed.
        Everything, your expression said,
was out of place,
        was not itself, was fragile

against sturdy oak trunks.
        It was a lie.
Exactly what I wanted
        to capture.

Didn't I Fuck You Once?

by Lillo Way

I've left the old Juilliard building,
am waiting for the #5 bus

in the dusk of my first October
in New York. Strolling by,

three trick-or-treaters smack me sideways,

swing me seasick, rout their hands
under my shirt, up my skirt, cup me —

heart-heaving me — in their newly-
adolescent hands. Above, the pious spire

of Riverside Church. Across, a noble-
ized soldier, high and white on his horse.

My two hands against their six.

Leotard and tights, sweat-glued,
keep them from my skin.

I writhe, the boys in cling,
into the empty-wide street.

If a car hits me, we'll all be hit.

But there are no cars. Not a soul
but the four of us and General Grant.

Not a sound but my huffs and oofs,
and the bells of the famous carillon.

Until, as they are lifting me off my feet,
the glorious accelerando of a bus.

They drop me and I land in a deep plié.

The doors whap open and I fall
into the belly of my savior.

A year later, I'm outside the great gates
of Barnard, piercing a stream of humans

erupting out the 116th Street exit from
the subworld. Our eyes meet and hold.

The leader of the trio, now fully a teenager.

He swerves to pass me close, and when
the sleeve of his jacket brushes mine

and his mouth isn't far from my ear,
he hiss-whispers the title of this poem.

Mama Bruja

by Cat Huang

Muchas gracias a AYLEEN SÁNCHEZ,
GERMAN DIAZ, SAMI FAUSTINO
y FRANCO ZACHARZEWSKI.

THANK YOU FOR SHARING YOUR
CULTURE & LANGUAGE WITH ME.
WITHOUT YOU ALL, THIS STORY WOULD
NOT HAVE BEEN POSSIBLE.

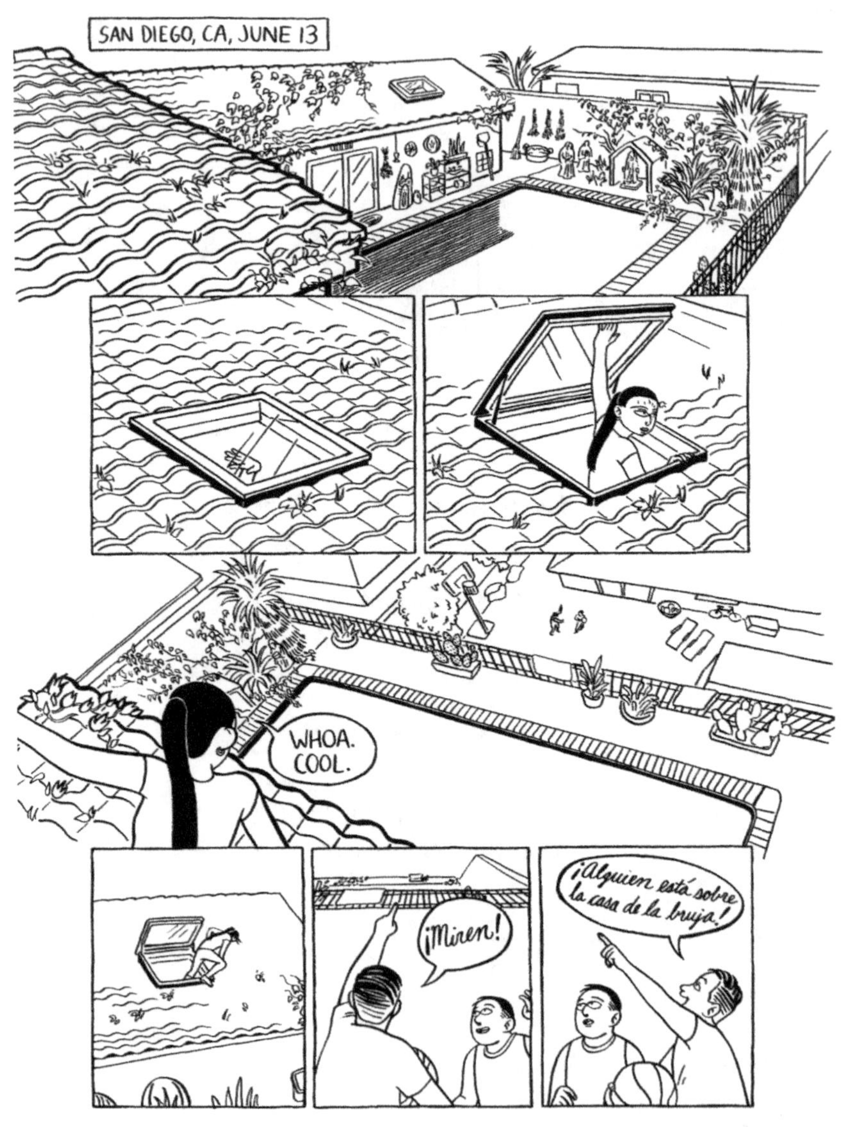
SAN DIEGO, CA, JUNE 13
WHOA. COOL.
¡Miren!
¡Alguien está sobre la casa de la bruja!

¡Oye! ¡Salta!
UM... WHAT?
¡Salta! JUMP IN THE bruja's POOL!
¡Salta!
¡Salta!
¡Salta!
¡Salta!
¡Salta!
¡Salta!
¡Salta!
ANTONIAAAA!
¡Salta!
¡Salta!
HI SOFÍA...
BE CAREFUL!!
UNLESS YOU WANT TO CLEAN WINDOWS WHILE I'M GONE, YOU HAVE NO BUSINESS UP THERE.
POOR SOFÍA ISN'T PAID ENOUGH TO TAKE CARE OF TWO PEOPLE YOU KNOW.
SOFÍA, WHAT DOES "BRUJA" MEAN?
WERE YOU TALKING TO THE BOYS NEXT DOOR? DON'T LISTEN TO THEM. THEIR ONLY HOBBY IS THROWING THINGS OVER THE FENCE.

¡Ven! GUADALUPE ASKED ME TO MAKE YOU BIRTHDAY CAKE.
COME, COME!
HOLA ABUELITA!
Hola mija.
CALL HER Mama Lupe.
ABUELITA? MAMÁ?
NOT MAMÁ. Máma.
Mama Lupe. BECAUSE IN THIS HOUSE, GUADALUPE IS YOUR MAMA.

TODAY WE WILL CELEBRATE A LOT!
Feliz Cumpleaños Antonia!
YOU HAVE ANOTHER MAMA, YOU ARE ONE STEP CLOSER TO BEING A WOMAN, AND I GET A FEW WEEKS OF VACATION, HAHA!
I SWEAR, IF YOU SEND ME TO ANOTHER MATH BOOT CAMP, IT'D BE SUCH A WASTE. I FLUNKED LAST TIME. LOWEST SCORE!
I KNOW. I DON'T KNOW HOW TO DEAL WITH YOU. I MAY START COPYING YOUR GRANDMA AND PRAY.
ooOooOH MARY AND JESUS...
PLEASE MAKE MY DAUGHTER NORMAL AND NOT AN EMBARRASSMENT.
GUADALUPE IS THRILLED TO FINALLY SEE YOU. IF YOU COME NEXT SUMMER TOO, SHE'LL GIVE YOU A HUGE QUINCEAÑERA!
OH NO, SHE DOESN'T HAVE TO. I DON'T KNOW ANY OF THE CUSTOMS, I'D HATE TO DISAPPOINT.
PRAY WHATEVER THE HELL YOU WANT, I'M A LOST CAUSE.
YOU WANT ME TO BE PERFECT, BUT I SUCK AT EVERYTHING YOU MAKE ME DO. WHY CAN'T I BE ME? I NEED A BREAK.

EVEN IF ONLY YOUR Mama Lupe IS MEXICAN, la sangre está en tus venas.
YOU ARE MORE MEXICAN THAN YOU THINK, ANTONIA.
I MEAN... I DON'T REALLY KNOW WHY I SUDDENLY WANTED TO COME HERE.
ya viene amaneciendo
ya la lu... dio
BUT I'M HAPPY TO SEE ABUE...MAMA LUPE.
Levántate de maña...
mira que ya amanec...
BEEP BEEP BEEP BEEP
BEEP
BEEP
BEEP
7:50
Thursday June 14
Alarm
Snooze again?
BEEP BEEP
BEEP BEEP
SHIT!
MATH
SOFÍA'S INSTRUCTIONS: WAKE UP EVERYDAY AT 7:30AM.
HOLA MAMA LUPE!
Hola mija.
MATH CAMP

BOIL EGGS FOR BREAKFAST.
UGH, I'M SORRY. I'VE NEVER USED A GAS STOVE. WHY WON'T IT WORK??
Presionas y la giras.
ALWAYS USE THE TORTILLA BASKET FOR EVERY MEAL.
SO IT'S A STAPLE...LIKE RICE FOR ASIANS.
WASH DISHES.
...WHAT? I WASHED IT...
¡No puedes dejar la sartén mojada!
SHE LIKES MAKING MOLE. DON'T TOUCH THE POT UNLESS SHE ASKS YOU TO.
THAT'S SO MUCH WORK...
HELP GUADALUPE WITH WHATEVER CHORES SHE WANTS.
DOES SHE BUY EVERY VIRGIN MARY SHE SEES?!
ABOVE ALL, EXPLORE THE HOME AND HAVE FUN.
TAP TAP TAP TAP
¿Antonia?
¿Por qué andas siempre en tu teléfono, sin llamar a nadie?
HM? WHAT?

¡Dame eso, ve afuera a jugar!
WAIT, WHAT?
¡Afuera! ¡Juega!
Tengo que ver la misa en la televisión.
CLACK
HUH??
¡Oye!
SPLISH
ARE YOU A MINI bruja?
DO YOU LIVE HERE NOW? HELLOOOOOOOOO?
HEY!!
WHAT'S A "BRUJA"?
WITCH. YOU LIVE IN THE WITCH'S HOME.
WHERE'D YOU GET THAT IDEA?
I'LL TELL YOU IF YOU JUMP IN THE POOL.
ONLY IF YOU TELL ME WHY YOU WANT ME TO.

OK WELL... IT'S THE bruja's SECRET PORTAL.
SHE USED IT TO LIVE MANY DIFFERENT LIVES.
IT'S THE ONLY POOL IN THIS ENTIRE NEIGHBORHOOD AND NO ONE'S ALLOWED IN IT. WHEN YOU JUMP IN, YOU COME OUT AS A DIFFERENT PERSON IN A DIFFERENT WORLD.
THE HIGHER THE JUMP, THE BIGGER THE DIFFERENCE. I'M SURPRISED YOU DON'T KNOW THIS, MINI bruja.
HEY, I'M NOT A WITCH!
YOU LIVE ALONE IN THAT BIG HOUSE WITH THE bruja AND NO OTHER FAMILY! YOU HELP HER WITH HER WEIRD POTION POT EVERYDAY!
WELL... WELL I'M NOT WEIRD LIKE THAT, OK?? I'M NORMAL.
No manches! I'M SURE YOU'RE A bruja.
WELL, ANYWAYS! MY NAME'S TONI. WHAT'S YOURS?
I'M GABRIEL. WANNA ADD ME ON SNAPCHAT?
SHOOT, I'M GONNA NEED MY PHONE... I'LL BE RIGHT BACK.

MAMA LUPE?
Por eso, Padre, te pedimos que santifiques
mismo Espíritu...
MAMA LUPE?
MAMA LUPEEE??
MAM-? AH!
BZZT BZZT
DICCIONARIO Español-Inglés
Andrew y Guadalupe
de luna de miel en
lago Xochimilco
DICCIONARIO
Español-

ANDREW AND GUADALUPE!
MADRE
IT'S ABUELITO!
WHAT! WHICH ONE IS MAMA LUPE?
GUADALUPE AT 15?!
Andrew 12 años
Guadalupe, Ofelia, Angélica y madre Carmen Amézcua
Guadalupe 15 años

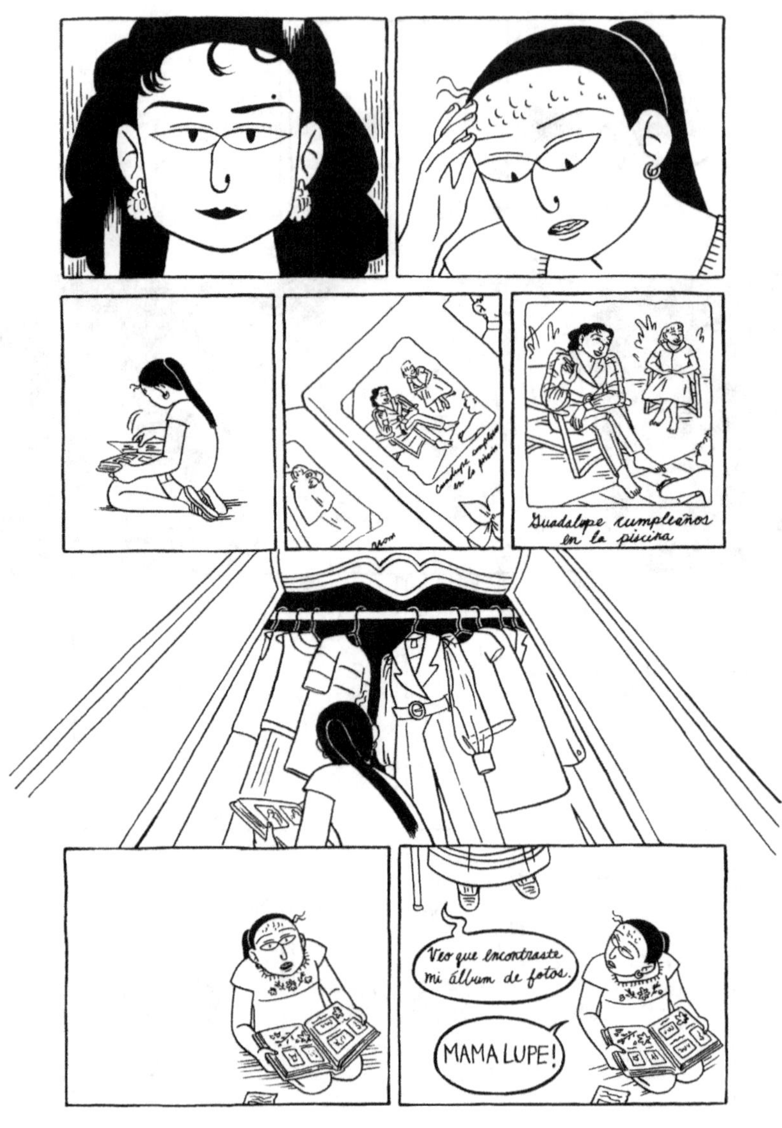
Guadalupe cumpleaños
en la piscina
Veo que encontraste
mi álbum de fotos.
MAMA LUPE!

YOU LOOK SO BEAUTIFUL AND CONFIDENT HERE!
WILL I GROW UP TO BE LIKE YOU?
Cuando tu Abuelito falleció y mi única hija se fue, yo continué viviendo mi vida, pero por dentro estaba perdida. Mi vida cambió tanto, y nadie estuvo allí para acompañarme.
Los caminos de Dios son un misterio. Mi familia no me ha dejado deambulando por siempre porque mi nieta ha regresado.
Aún así, Él me la envía como una errante.
No estarás sola como lo estuve yo.
Sé que el cambio asustará, pero tengo la oportunidad de ser para ti lo que yo no pude tener.

I CAN'T...
I CAN'T UNDERSTAND WHAT YOU'RE SAYING.
Antonia, eres una niña buena e inteligente. Pronto cambiarás y te convertirás en una mujer.
I DON'T KNOW!!
Quizás no lo sepas, pero tu potencial es infinito.
I'M SORRY I'M SO EMBARRASSING.
Veo tanto de mí en ti. No tienes de que preocuparte.
Lo veo todo tan claro.
Tienes un gran futuro por delante, y yo estaré ahí para guiarte.
Quizás sea mi edad ¡pero ahora todo es tan bello! Y tú eres la cosa más bella de todas.
Yo te guiaré.

A MONTH LATER
I SEE... THANK YOU. BYE.
CLAK
ANTONIA?
SHE... DIDN'T MAKE IT.
I'M SORRY. ARE YOU ALRIGHT?
TE QUIERO MUCHO
I DON'T KNOW. NO ONE I KNEW HAS EVER DIED BEFORE. WHAT DO I DO?
I'M SORRY FOR YOUR LOSS. YOUR MAMÁ IS FLYING OVER SOON.
WE WILL TAKE CARE OF EVERYTHING. YOU MUST BE HEARTBROKEN.
TE QUIERO

FLOOM
CRRK CRRK
Yo te guiaré.

SKREEEE
¡Hola! YOU MUST BE ANTONIA'S MAMÁ YES?
HI, YEAH. WHERE IS SHE?
I THINK SHE'S IN THE BACKYARD.
ANTONIAAA?
¡Salta!
¡Hazlo!
ANTONIA??
¡Hazlo! ¡Salta!
¡¡Salta, salta!!

ANTONIA?! WHAT ARE YOU DOING??
ANTONIA?!
GET DOWN THIS INSTANT!!
DO IT MINI bruja!!
¡¡Hazlo! ¡¡Salta!!
GET DOWN!!
DO WHAT I SAY!!
¡Salta!
¡Salta!
¡Salta!
YOU DON'T KNOW WHAT YOU'RE DOING
YOU'RE EMBARRASSING ME
YOU LOOK RIDICULOUS!
IT'S DANGER
ONIA LEASE!
¡Salta!
DON YOU
LA BRUJA...

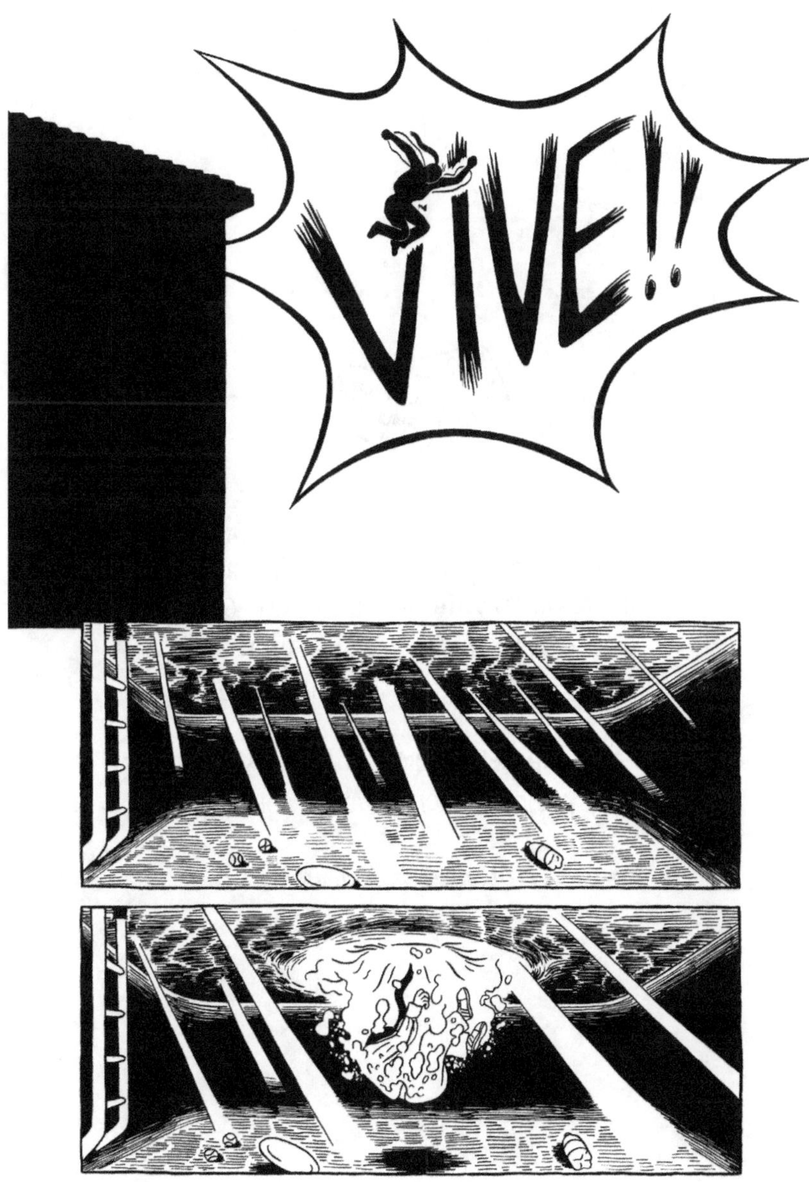
VIVE!!

THIS STORY IS ONE PART IN A LARGER
COLLABORATION WITH THE "FULL CIRCLE" GROUP:
CLAIRE WYMAN, SABRINA FUTCH,
REBECCA TURBEE, & JOSH FOLTZ,

WITH HELP FROM OUR ADVISORS,
R. KIKUO JOHNSON & TAYLOR POLITES.

¡Gracias a todos!

Aprons

by Carol Iaciofano Aucoin

After my mother's death, my sisters and brother and I embarked on a task
familiar to many adult children: clearing out our childhood home. My
father had died a few years before. The house my parents had shared since
1957 was a set-in-amber archive of family photos, letters, recipes, books,
clothes, and tools.

We unearthed a trove of artifacts from our middle class, mid-twentieth
century life: formal gloves used for church, glass-lidded CorningWare cas-
seroles with their signature blue and white cornflower design, and portable
transistor radios that had magically connected us to Top Forty songs. Each
item carried its own story for me, unspooling a resonant internal movie.

Even so, I was surprised by a drawerful of aprons, a stack of memories col-
orful and neatly folded. Some were jewel-toned taffeta that my mother had
worn for elegant dinners served to a houseful of guests. Some were cotton
in florals and plaids, which I'd worn as a very young child helping her make
cinnamon rolls, chocolate cake, homemade pasta. Back then, putting on an
apron was as much a part of the pre-baking ritual as washing your hands.
These aprons, tucked away for decades, prompted a tumble of feelings way
beyond their form or function.

The female apron-wearers in my large extended Italian Catholic family
were a mix of mostly housewives and some working mothers, and each
one was an exquisitely talented domestic artist. They all cooked fabulously
and seemingly continuously. During my formative years in the 1950s and
1960s, takeout food was an occasional treat in our family, not a dinner
fallback option. An apron was as essential a tool as their hand-held mixer

or upright vacuum cleaner.

Like cooking, laundry requires time and measurements. A competent housewife would know how to allocate portions; how to make things last. An apron could significantly reduce the amount of clothing in the laundry basket, on the clothesline, in the mending pile, at the ironing board. An apron could create extra free time: to talk on the phone, finish a cigarette, drink a cup of coffee while it was still warm. Then in the 1970s, as the second wave of feminism crested, the apron changed from useful accessory to badge of oppression of the women who devoted their lives to making other lives easier. As in any new movement that encounters heavy pushback, lines were initially drawn sharply to delineate new ground. Because kitchen expertise was a fundamental component of the middle-class housewife role, its luster faded. The modern woman needed to have bigger priorities than checking an oven timer.

In my mother I had the best culinary teacher a daughter could hope for, but by the time I entered high school I'd lost my appetite for the skills that underpinned a flaky pie crust or ensured that veal scallopini turned out both tender and crispy. Although I still liked the process of cooking, I began to view it as a lesser, disposable craft. Where before I had marveled at the magic my mother and aunts spun in creating abundant family feasts, now I only saw all the effort beforehand, and for all of that, how none of the finished product lasted a long time in the way that building a cabinet or fixing a car did (see: traditional work, male).

I also couldn't help noticing that even on the day of a party, my mother and aunts never truly relaxed. They were lively participants in all the overlapping conversations. But it was only the women who monitored how much food was left in the serving platters, only the women who continually left the table to refill coffees or to whip cream for desserts, only the women who organized the (female) cousins to wrap up leftovers for everyone to take home.

Cooking and baking seemed the ignore-at-your-peril fine print of Happily
Ever After: if I got skilled at the stove, I'd always be at the stove. It felt safer
to help out by doing the more neutral tasks of setting the table or washing
the dishes. I kept my blasphemous opinion to myself; it was simpler to
become the one kid in our family who just didn't like cooking. Simpler, but
not easier; I knew my mother was baffled and more than a little sad that
I had abruptly lost interest in something she not only held dear, but was
justifiably proud of. I also felt guilty because, of course, I continued to bene-
fit from her gourmet cooking skills, not the least being part of a household
known among my friends for always welcoming guests to our bountiful
weeknight dinners.

It wasn't until I had my first apartment after college that my kitchen phobia
began to evaporate. This was partly pragmatic: unless I mastered even a
few recipes, I'd eat through most of my new paycheck in takeout food. My
dormant cooking interest re-awoke in a surprisingly strong way and with
it came a new recreational activity of devising menus for myself and to host
friends.

On trips home, my mother and I began to spend part of the visit cooking together, with her happily, belatedly sharing epicurean wisdom. She
viewed my newfound culinary interest as another life phase, like a hobby
taken up when young, dropped, and then picked up again as an adult. (I
remember that at that point we used aprons only for baking; a stray drop of
sauce on clothing could be easily dispatched, but puffs of flour on a sweater
or pants was too annoying to contemplate.)

I began to replace my smaller truth, the dismay at a table's worth of food
quickly disappearing, with a larger truth: home-cooked food is often a key
ingredient to forging enduring memories with family and friends. This

seems a blindingly obvious statement, now; forty years ago, it felt like a thorny one.

When I became a mother of two kids, I did indeed spend countless hours in the kitchen, and juggled work and domestic duties like every other mother I knew. As glad as I was to have more professional opportunities than my mother had known, I was also aware that at the end of a work day the symbolic, if not the actual, apron awaited. My husband, never a cook, does kitchen cleanup. It's an efficient division of labor, though not an equal one. Cleanup is nowhere near as fun as cooking, but it is not time-sensitive: there is no meal planning or meal prep involved, interweaved with kids' activities and business meetings.

In the 1990s, some forward-thinking tech companies had evolved enough to allow working at home for part of the week. On my at-home days, I scheduled my work across daytime and evening hours, alternating that with pre-dinner tasks of chopping vegetables or preparing pasta sauce, or family baking time, with our dining room table covered with flour, our kids kneeling on chairs mixing cookie batter or frosting cupcakes. I've saved their little smock aprons; mementos of afternoons both busy and cozy.

It was during these years, long after I'd first edged back to the stove, that cooking finally became an uncomplicated and satisfying aspect of my life. If I was now in part defined by the meals I created, that part turned out to be expansive, not constrictive.

Our son and daughter, now adults, consider the kitchen, simply, a place of food; not a trap or a cultural symbol. Our daughter is an especially creative cook; unlike the younger me, she has never considered cooking an either/or option for how to manage her professional and personal life. She and her brother came of age in an era where men as well as women have food blogs and compete in TV cooking or baking shows. For them and their friends, food prep is unyoked from gender roles; it can be a basic daily activity, or transformed into sport, or elevated into art. No apron required.

I still cook and bake wearing just everyday clothes, but occasionally I take out one of the vintage designs I've saved from my mother's apron collection. On a recent Sunday afternoon, getting ready to make a batch of her wine biscuits, I selected a floral cotton of pale pink and green and yellow. I began the pre-baking ritual. I washed my hands. I put on the apron, and shaped the long ties into a bow, my mother's hands once again guiding my own.

On Seeing You, My Son, Overmedicated for the First Time

by Christine Jones

I drive us through the drive-thru
& you misaim the fries to your mouth;

flimsy, undercooked strands dropping
on your lap, in the crack beside the door —

that impossible place to reach. Not like
how you once straddled my shoulders &

I held your knees as you stretched
to grab hold of the dogwood branch

for a closer look at fledglings, begging,
as you did then, too, for fast food.

You tell me you're fine. But you look like
the blue jay in the refuge I extended twigs to.

Through a chain-link fence, offerings added
to its harbored nest while it waits to heal.

And while you sleep, I sweep the car seat, the mat,
toss uneaten fries outside where another bird flies,

claims one & flits back to the forsythia bush
below your window, a stubbled spray of pale buds.

White Hair

by Nancy Agabian

My mother's hair is white. Bright white, like the inside of a mussel shell, iridescent. Fine lines on a pink scalp. But only for an inch. Where the white roots end the brown hair dye begins, demarcating a continental divide. Mom hides the white drift under a fuzzy black bowler hat. Her hair, tucked behind her ears, has grown so long in the back that the white, blond, and brown threads are mixing, like silk poking out from the ears of corn neglected in my parents' vegetable drawer. Sometimes a few wisps fly loose in front of her face but she doesn't push them away. In my childhood her sleek brown hair curled into full dollops, shaped by pincurls she set at night and fixed with spray during the day, never falling into her face ever. The contrast between then and now is another sign of her social graces slipping away, like when she belches loudly and announces, "That felt good!" The mechanisms that have always kept her in check are disintegrating.

It's early November and I'm on a weekend visit that I make every two weeks to help my elderly parents in their Boston suburb. When I arrive, I assemble my list of the usual tasks: grocery shop, laundry, pay bills. Mom's hair makes it to the top of the list. Dad confides in me that they're at a loss over what to do. He's been known to help my mom dye her hair from a box when she can't make it to the beauty salon, but those days are over. Multi-step tasks like cooking and cleaning have become difficult for them. Dad has a bit more capacity than she does: he is still driving short trips nearby though never at night. Mom stopped driving a few months ago, unaware that our family conspired to take her keys away, replacing them with a set to a long-gone Toyota Camry. I had tried a more direct approach but it didn't work:

"You can't drive, Mom."
"Why not?"
"You've lost your short term memory."
"Oh please. That's just normal aging."
"Not according to the doctor. You have mild cognitive impairment."
"I was never tested for that!"
"Yes, you were. The doctor asked you questions for half an hour. He said
you shouldn't drive."
"I don't remember that."
"Exactly!"
"You listen to me: I've never had an accident, not once!"

She had a point, but it's also true that the last time I got in a car with her,
she straddled the broken white line and forgot where to turn for Stop &
Shop, bumping over a curb. I was terrified, but my mother was never the
type who could admit she was wrong, and now her denial was actually
a symptom of the disease. I stopped arguing since she only drove once a
month to Madeline's salon anyway.

But now that we've replaced her keys with the phony set, she has stopped
going altogether, and though I am relieved for her safety, it is painful to see
my mother lose her capability. That line on her head is a chasm — in slid
her memory for quotidian things, like what she wants to order off a menu,
where she went today, and whether or not she called me that evening,
but it has also engulfed parts of her persona in the process. Originally an
elementary school teacher before becoming a mother, she volunteered at a
small art museum throughout my childhood. Her docent card granted her
free admission to local art museums, which we frequently visited; she also
took me to theater, dance, and concerts, gifting me with a cultural education that couldn't be had in my public school. She saw the lack and pitched
herself as a cultural coordinator for the entire school system, landing her
dream job. Here was a vibrant, gregarious woman who would flash her

bright smile as she said hello to everyone in the room, who struck up conversations with strangers and asked incisive questions when they were taken from the audience, who remembered to send cards to friends when they were sick or lost someone. Now, when she and my father frequent the nearby restaurants that appeal to the geriatric crowd, she bemoans that she never runs into anyone she knows. Most of the time she stays home, watching CNN on its continual loop, scanning *Reader's Digest,* and forgetting the cup of water she put in the microwave to make tea.

It won't be easy to take her to the hair salon. Though she is no longer independent, she is more independent-minded now than ever: in her imagination she is still her full self, complete with a head of brown hair.

***

When Mom takes off her hat, Madeline says, "Oh my goodness." It's a Saturday afternoon and the salon is full of elder white women. "Your hair is almost as long as mine!" Madeline says, making a quick save, staying silent on the continental divide. She has beautiful hair: full and long, a chocolate brown strewn with honey highlights.

When my mother says she wants her hair colored, Madeline tells her there's not enough time in the schedule.

"Why don't you get it cut today and have it colored another time," I offer, knowing she can't maintain a schedule of regular dye jobs.

"You might even want to keep it white," Madeline says, gently taking her by the hand to her chair.

Thankfully, my mother agrees. She'd been anxious this morning, asking repeatedly about where we were going, who she was seeing and at what time.

Hemming and hawing in her light blue bathrobe worn crookedly over her tiny frame, she hadn't felt like going. I finally convinced her to dress and get in the car by reassuring her that we were seeing Madeline. Then as I drove, she kept asking if I knew the address. I let her give me directions to the center of town: long term memories seem unscathed, firmly rooted on one side of the continent. When I parked the car, she demanded, "Don't tell her how to cut my hair!"

It would be out of character for me to do so, but Mom must have felt a loss of control — after all, I had made the appointment. Perhaps it's not unlike what she felt when I cut my hair as a teenager — coming home one day with one side short and one side long, the front bleached with an amber streak. I was no longer the little girl whose thick, long black hair she brushed out from snarls and braided every morning. "Oh my god, I can't take you with me anywhere now!" Mom exclaimed.

But she never did stop bringing me with her to shop at Filene's Basement, to attend Sts Sahag and Mesrob church, to explore Isabella Stewart Gardner's villa, and to see Lily Tomlin search for signs of intelligent life at the Wang Center. The rest of my appearance was subject to intense scrutiny and dragged into bargaining sessions, however. I couldn't wear my jean jacket with the honeycomb bleached into the back (in homage to Sting) because of my crazy hair. Well, then, I retorted, she would have to buy me the oversized tweed coat at Syms instead. Appearance thus disrupted our relationship, teaching me a damning lesson. Sylvia was a striking woman with full, well-balanced features, dark hair and light skin; I resembled her but my nose more prominent, my smile thrust into overbite, my skin an earthier tone. I could never live up to her conventional beauty, nor to her standards. Appearance was the seat of her power as an Armenian American woman who came of age during the Fifties — from the care she took matching her pantsuit to the color of her lipstick to the style of her costume jewelry. Yielding to an atmospheric pressure, she assimilated to whiteness and conformed to strict gender roles. It wasn't just crucial to look good in order to get ahead and get what you wanted; to fail the standard of beauty could mean a stumble in society. This was the message I had absorbed, anyway.

After twenty minutes of snipping, Madeline calls me over. From behind, Mom's hair is a pretty heart shape, cut close to her neck. When I step between her and the mirror, I look into her face, and I'm astonished. I thought this was the right thing to do, so I'm not prepared to feel a wave of regret. Mom's hair is white. She looks *old*: frail and fragile. And yet somehow resolute. In her smock, without her arms, she looks like she's strapped into a toboggan, ready to fly down a mountain.

"It looks nice!" I chirp, and Madeline confirms: "People pay to get this kind of bright white hair." When Mom doesn't look convinced, Madeline adds, "It's like your daughter's hair now. Look at how pretty her hair is."

I turn to look in the mirror. My hair is gray. Not white. I get what Madeline's trying to do. But I'm disoriented.

For all my life, Mom's hair and eyes have been dark like mine. Sometimes, against my wishes, looking at her felt like seeing my own reflection. Here now, standing with my back to the salon's mirror, I try to read her face, familiar in her deep brown eyes, foreign with this new cushion of fluffy cloud. She smiles nervously, and I can't read her expression, if she's angry or surrendering. Growing up, she was a master of masks, putting on one image to the public while showing a very different one at home, like answering the phone with a perfect, chiming hello immediately after screaming her head off. I expect that I will catch shit from her later.

Though it's new for me to bring my mother to the hair salon, it is also true that I have been invested in her appearance long before this day. Beyond how she looked, my mother led a full, busy life. Sometimes she was late dying her hair, so her roots would show, and brat that I was, I told her that it looked terrible, that she was a phony and that I would never dye my hair like her. *Ever.*

Now I'm fifty and nature has found me. My hairdresser has suggested I get lowlights, but I like the silver. It's also true that I've held onto my teenage oath. I didn't want to be like my mother; I thought her vain, too concerned with appearance, with *my* appearance. I once had to flee to a stall in the church bathroom, crying silently into my hands, when she didn't like how I looked, damning my "sad sack face" at an Armenian Church Youth of America dance. I just wanted my mother to be real with me, unknowingly aching for some kind of intimacy. To seek it, I ran far away from home to Los Angeles and then New York, finding community through poetry and performance. My appearance was composed of homemade costumes of crocheted hot pants, thrift store white gloves, and faux fur wings. I let my hair grow long into waves and wove it into braids; at other times I shaved it close to my skull: my own queer beauty. Underneath this carefully crafted sense of self, however, loomed a dormant fear: to be in proximity of my mother's orbit, within her sphere of control, would be the end of me.

Now my mother is frail and elderly, and I need to care for her. I don't know what I'm more terrified by: breaking my old promise to myself and thereby doing myself in. Or that I'm losing my mom, especially the problematic parts of her personality that have shaped me. Or that I am growing old myself. Here I am, ironically, imposing a standard of appearance on her that she once insisted of me.

When we get home from the salon, Mom won't blame me for her white hair, but she won't thank me either — not surprisingly, the episode will soon be erased from her memory banks. It seems there is no need for me to fear. The mask she was forced to wear to appear acceptable to strangers

— and that had made me feel so abandoned — is now sloughing away with her social graces. Though she is barreling away from her former self, some of the things that she had held on to so tightly are now tumbling into the chasm — and it may be a blessing.

Before we leave the salon, Mom writes out a check, and Madeline asks if she is still driving.

"Oh yes," Mom answers. Does she honestly believe she is still actively behind the wheel? Or is her mask resurfacing to protect her dignity?

It doesn't matter. I had always conceived of the continental divide as some kind of tectonic boundary, a rift where plateaus collide. In reality, it's the point along the mountaintops from which raindrops drain in opposite directions: the east towards the Atlantic, the west towards the Pacific. Streams rush to rivers that fill the oceans, their currents eventually connecting somewhere on earth. Somehow my mother and I have bridged our imaginary chasm, the echoing chambers, between our current and former selves.

Madeline catches on. "Sometimes it's a relief not to drive, right?" she replies, smiling and winking at me.

with what letters remain

by Christopher Porcaro

…because even the soul is a creature…"
– Meister Eckhart

you're here,
telling me how
a disease survives
in saliva & blood & water
& its swift mutation
to rancid wine in
cursed wine hide-
common-wells where
each of us enters
a soft drowning. i
drive my four-wheel
leviathan west on sunset
toward nuclear tide
& stop at an end.
your cigarette blues
with formaldehyde,
flame retardant & hand
cleaner. "is radiation
coming across
this sea?" she exhales.
a dissonance reborn
in the back of her throat
we exchange dry bones
whittled to tuning rods
& stuff them with marrow.

tomorrow, she widens
her thighs &
dreams, "here's a chain-
mail hood my brother
left." rusted, but
stronger with redox
from some crusade
"it was his
forced oxidation,
bringing him closer
to sublime ecdysis."
he died suffocating
and alone before
this new disease
suffocates alone
we sew each other's
bones to our own
& pray the graft takes.
while we wait
i read, burning
in white text on night
-rich sheet,
annotation resistant:
she says she thinks
we're all segments
of a Whole re-
arranged to near
-infinity to forget
each other's face &
she's right, there's
only suffering to hold
us together.
& forgetting

Divertimento

by Jessica Treadway

Half past noon on a weekday, the middle of summer. Sunny and hot. The flags outside the municipal buildings sway not in the least, which is a way of saying that the air is as still as it can possibly be — not even the premonition of a breeze, even for those who have premonitions.

In the historic part of the city, two women are having lunch on one of the benches surrounding a public playground. Now when I say "bench," you may be picturing a strictly utilitarian apparatus, backless and with a hard slab for a seat. But in fact, these benches are nearly like sofas. They've been designed with more than mere utility in mind: they are for parents and teachers who need a place to sit while they supervise children on seesaws and monkey bars; retirees who come here to read, or to remind themselves of the world they used to inhabit; and working people like Ann and Petra who meet once in a while on their lunch break, who prefer to do so outdoors when the weather is good, and whose experience of their hour together is enhanced many times over by the fact that they can share the wide, curved, cushiony surface made of a soft yet indestructible polymer and, when they tire of sitting upright, lean against a backrest of the same material, placed at just the right distance and angle in relation to the seat. (At the unveiling, dozens of toss pillows provided color and decoration, but those have of course long since disappeared.) And yes, since you may be wondering, there are armrests, too.

When the benches first appeared, replacing the old, hard, backless ones, the two women remarked almost every time they met about how amazing it was: such a treat, so unexpected. But that was a number of years ago. It's been ages since they've mentioned it, now.

The women are not young anymore — that's important to know. They're not all that far from retirement. Neither of them likes to think about this too much, though for different reasons.

Petra has brought her usual: a sandwich, chips, and an apple packed from home. Ann always buys her lunch from one of the many vendors lining the cobblestone path leading to the playground, which lies almost exactly halfway between the buildings in which the women work. Petra has a more important and higher-paying job than Ann, although Ann likes her job more than Petra likes hers.

Today Ann has picked up souvlaki, which she unwraps slowly after she and Petra greet each other and sit down. It is only with Petra that she chooses what to her are exotic foods, even though Petra's own exoticism (owing mostly to the foreignness of her name) has worn off. Petra has no way of knowing it, but Ann is considering putting an end to these lunches, occasional though they are. The past few times — well, more than that, really — Petra's mood has been dark, and her energy low, and it really does Ann no good at all to be around her. It was one thing at the beginning, when she was kind of fascinated by Petra's worldliness. But now it's just, frankly, a drag.

Ann feels guilty for thinking this way, because if she were a true friend, wouldn't she ask Petra if something was wrong? And if she could help?

But it doesn't actually feel like true friendship. They met at the fiftieth birthday dinner of a mutual friend, and discovered they worked near each other. These lunches started out pleasant enough, and it's convenient, but nothing more. If Ann weren't already in the city because of her job, and taking a break at midday anyway, she wouldn't be meeting Petra for lunch or anything else.

A red rubber ball rolls near their feet, and one of the children from the playground calls to ask if they will send it back over the fence. Petra either hasn't heard the request or is pretending not to have heard it, so Ann puts down her souvlaki, picks up the ball, and drop-kicks it back to where the children are waiting. A few of the kids snicker, old enough to be amused by the sight of a woman who could be their grandmother kicking a ball with the toe of her pointy, professional shoe.

But they would also have to admit to feeling impressed that she kicked it so well. Surely, firmly, and confident in her aim. In fact, one of the boys will remember this image for most of his life, usually when he is called upon for courage — to do something he is afraid of and thinks he cannot do.

When Ann sits back down to resume eating her sandwich, Petra tells her "I'm no good at sports," as if this has to do with anything.

And something in what she sees in her "friend" then — the slump of Petra's shoulders, the frown in her brow — causes Ann to snap, as it were, and she smashes the slim but substantial wall, the one made of politeness, that has always existed between them. "What is the matter with you? I haven't seen you smile in months. I'm telling you, it's too much… lately when I go back to work after seeing you, I have a bad afternoon, or I just about fall asleep at my desk."

None of this seems to surprise Petra, which surprises Ann. Does this mean she could or should have said something sooner? Petra looks not surprised, but even sadder than she did before. "I tried to throw the ball back once," she explains, "and it hit the top of the fence and punctured on one of those metal spikes. The kids laughed. Some of them even booed."

"So what? They're children."

Petra shakes her head. "You don't understand. When you're sensitive, everything cuts the same, whether it's big or little."

Ann keeps herself from speaking the phrase that occurs to her, which is *pity party.*

Petra says, "I read a lot of books" as if this has to do with anything.

"… ?" Now Ann is the one who frowns, fumbling for a response. "Well, that's good, isn't it? It's great that you read books. Too many people don't." *I don't,* she doesn't add, because it dismays her that this has become the case.

"But is it great?" Petra shades her eyes against the sun. "I've been reading things lately, the Russians, that make me think I should be looking for a different kind of book. Books that don't ask questions. Books that don't make me think. Maybe I would be happier."

"… ?" Again, Ann can think of nothing to offer by way of following up.

"They talk a lot about the meaning of life. Whether life has any meaning. Take the one I'm reading now." Petra reaches into her bag to pull out a paperback. "Basically, the author says that everything we do, every action we take, is only aimed at distracting us from the fact that it all ends in death."

"A kind of 'Life sucks and then you die' kind of thing?" As soon as it leaves her mouth Ann regrets her sarcasm, but luckily, Petra seems not to notice or to mind.

"Some of them seem to think that if life does have meaning," she concedes, "that meaning is love. The connections we make with other people. There's this one story about a woman who talks to her sugar bowl, it just sits there on her table and she becomes friends with it. I like that one a lot."

"Well, there you go! What's wrong with that?" Ann had not expected to hear so much relief in her own voice.

"That's easy for you to say — you have love."

Oh, dear. Is Petra asking Ann to say she loves her? She can't do it — it isn't true. But before she can figure out how to respond, Petra has reached over to grab her by the arm, almost as if she hasn't even realized it. Aside from the hugs they exchange when they meet and part each time — which, in the way of such things, are not really hugs — they have never touched each other. What is this?!

"Are you saying it hasn't happened to you, yet? Because I don't believe it. At our age it happens more often than not — the lying awake at night, wondering what you've done with your life, where all that time's gone, and how much you have left. And on top of that, wondering *What is the point?*"

Ann shakes off Petra's hand with more resentment and vigor than she would have liked to reveal. "What a cliché! And if you don't mind, I came here to have a nice lunch, not talk about dying!" She looks up at the clock on the bank tower, wishing she were back in her office instead of sitting on this bench next to Petra. Then she tells herself *Stop* — that isn't being mindful. It isn't being *here*. She's been advised that trying to be mindful, and here, will improve her experience of life. "Who says you have to believe what's in that book?" She nods at the paperback.

"I'm not sure what you're getting at," Petra says. She puts the other half of her sandwich away, as if the turn of their conversation has spoiled her appetite.

"I'm just saying that you could choose to have a different opinion. You could decide for yourself that life has any meaning you want." Ann is not entirely sure where she's going with this, but she likes the sound of it — she likes hearing something remotely intellectual, maybe even remotely profound, in her own voice. She licks the last of the yogurt sauce, which has a fancier name she always forgets, from her fingers. As usual, she neglected to pick up any napkins from the vendor's stand, and this makes her irritated at herself.

Petra feels her lips give off a brief but violent quiver, and wonders if Ann notices. Probably not, she decides. After all, they are sitting less across from each other than side by side, and she's never been particularly impressed by Ann's powers of perception.

But Ann has more on the ball than Petra gives her credit for. "You think those kids are worried about any of that?" Ann gestures widely toward the playground, upon which the sun has chosen to direct its strongest rays. "Whether life has any meaning? They couldn't care less."

Petra follows the track of Ann's hand, then shakes her head. "No. But that's exactly my point. They don't know about death, yet."

"Well, neither do you. Not really. You only know it in the abstract."

"What?!" Can Ann really be saying this? Petra hardly believes what she's hearing. "My father ran over that boy when I was in middle school —"

"I know, you've told me that story."

"— and I've watched both of my parents die… I took care of both of them at the end… I know death as well as anyone alive can know it!"

"And that's exactly my point." It feels good to Ann, being able to say this. Somehow, she realizes, she's always assumed that Petra's depression makes her the smarter of the two of them. Not so — right? At least, she is determined to divest herself of that idea. A person can be happy and smart at the same time. Though she knows people who would disagree with her, she refuses to believe that the two can't co-exist.

She must have murmured something without realizing, because Petra says, "What?"

Ann shakes her head. "I'm thinking of something I want to say to you, but I don't know whether it'll make you feel better or worse. It usually makes me feel better, but I think we might be different in that."

"What is it?" If Petra's trying to conceal the fact that she's intrigued — hopeful, even — it isn't working.

"It's from a sign on a Buddhist temple in Thailand."

"Wait — you've been to Thailand?"

How greatly Ann wishes to respond that yes, she has! How greatly she wishes for a single exotic experience of her own. Too late, she'd realized that of course Petra would ask. And how much Ann also wishes to avoid confessing the truth, which is that she saw the temple inscription only on social media.

But she prides herself more than anything on being a person who — despite being tempted, she's working on that — doesn't allow herself to put on airs that she hasn't earned. "No, it's just a post I saw, a photo, by someone I know who *did* go. Anyway, the sign over the door says 'Remember, one hundred years from now, all new people.'"

She draws out the last three words because they are, of course, the important ones. They are, after all, the point. Watching Petra's eyes, she can tell that it takes a moment for the meaning to sink in — as, Ann recalls, it did with her. Then she sees the click of Petra comprehending, before the dam finally gives way. "Why did you have to tell me that? Isn't that another way of saying that everything's irrelevant — whatever any of us do — because it will all be forgotten and we're all going to be replaced anyway? Doesn't it reinforce what those Russians are writing about, that none of it means anything?"

Though this has occurred to Ann herself, she's chosen to reject this interpretation. "No. What I'm saying, what it's saying, is that whatever we're worried or sad about, in the long run it's not a big deal. Doesn't that take some of the pressure off? Doesn't that make you feel... I don't know, lighter?"

But Petra's crying. For God's sake! Ann's not going to sit here and listen to that.

"I think you need to dwell in possibility," she continues, before Petra can deliver another morose rebuff. The phrase — *Dwell in possibility* — popped into Ann's head as she cast around for a path out of this pity party, though she could not name its source. Probably it is etched on one of the decorative stones a hippie friend of hers at work keeps in a shallow dish on her desk, for inspiration. *Believe. This too shall pass. The best is yet to come.*

"All these sayings. They're just so much hot air." Petra waves dismissively. At least she isn't crying anymore. She places the bag with her remaining half sandwich into her purse, as if preparing to take off. Ann would be fine — *more* than fine — with her leaving, but instead Petra says, "Tell me what you mean by 'possibility,'" sounding almost as if she might be doing Ann a favor by asking.

Once, at work, Ann was directed at the last minute to lead a meeting on a subject she knew nothing about. She feels that way now, forced to occupy the head of a table at which people sit waiting for her to educate them.

"Well, just look around you, it's everywhere," she says vaguely. The first thing she sees, looking around, is the playground. "One of those kids might grow up to do something remarkable, someday. More than one of them might. Invent something. Cure cancer."

"Oh, please. Why not just say, 'They're the hope of the future'? I mean really, talk about a cliché."

"Well, then, you might do something remarkable. You might feel something you never expected to feel." *Who's the hippie now?* she says then, but only inside her own head.

Petra has truly hoped for an answer she could hang her hat on. Instead what she gets is this mindless pablum about possibility… what a crock. "If we don't die of cancer, we'll just die of something else. And all those kids might just as easily end up homeless or on drugs. Or depressed, like me. At best they'll be automatons, living inside their phones like all the rest of them."

Why had she thought today might be different? She woke up thinking that something might come along to change her heart. But clearly, it isn't going to be lunch with Ann that does it.

By now, though, Ann has grown invested in convincing Petra. Or is it in convincing herself? And of what, again? Oh, right — the idea that life is worth living. That it all has meaning, even if we can't figure out what it is. That there's some purpose to being here.

Are those all the same, or three separate things?

"You're impossible!" she cries out. "Okay, if you need something less abstract, then take this bench."

"Mmmm?"

"This bench. How comfy it is. Remember how bad those old benches used to be? We almost stopped coming, we were going to meet somewhere else. But we couldn't decide where, so we came to the park one last time, and here was this new bench just waiting for us. You can see how much thought and care has gone into it. First, in the design. Then a prototype, which I'm sure the company tested on regular people like us. Asked them questions. Improved and adjusted things, according to the feedback they heard. Then produced them to spec, and installed them in this park, all so we could have a more comfortable place to sit while we eat our lunch and argue about whether anything in this world is worth doing, whether it has any meaning at all."

Saying this takes Ann's breath away. At work and at home, she hardly every utters more than one sentence at a time.

"You act as if they did it out of concern for us." Petra clutches her purse to her side even though she is still seated. "Purely for our comfort. When in fact, they did it for money."

"So? Why shouldn't they get paid for a job well done — for something that's useful to somebody else, or to the world? Would you do your job if you weren't getting paid? Of course not." Ann makes a more obnoxious sound than she intended, emphasizing this conclusion. To temper it she modulates her tone and adds, "My point is, there's always the possibility that something — a situation, a person, a mood — will change for the better."

"Or for the worse," Petra says.

"Well, of course, but the odds are fifty-fifty, aren't they? Why not anticipate they'll land on the 'better' side?" When Petra doesn't answer, Ann lets the momentum propel her forward. "Do you remember how it used to feel, sitting here? My butt would get numb. Now, it's practically like sitting on a couch in my own living room. It's made a difference in my life, this bench, and in yours, too, whether you admit it or not."

Petra admits, "Yes, it has made a difference." Her voice is little more than a murmur, but it's loud enough to be heard. "This moment right now is better for us than it would be, if not for this bench."

She's almost got it, Ann thinks. What she feels creeping up to her comprehension, what she wants to express. The answer to Petra's question: Tell me what you mean by *possibility.*

But now, interrupting, comes the same red rubber ball from the playground, rolling again at their feet. The kids clamor at the fence as they did the last time, calling for the women to send it back. "Your turn this time," Ann says, annoyed that the ball has bounced the insight — the revelation? — straight out of her head.

"But they'll laugh at me."

"If you don't try, how will you find out? Maybe this time they won't."

Petra smiles the smile of someone who knows better, picks up the ball, takes a few steps toward the playground, and tosses it as high as she can. To her surprise, it lands precisely in front of the child who'd kicked it by accident out of bounds, a first-grader who bullies kids his own age but — because he has been punished for doing otherwise — will, for another year or two beyond now, treat adults with the respect he's been told they deserve. "Thanks, lady!" he shouts, picking it up before running back to his friends.

"That means nothing," Petra tells Ann, returning to the bench. "That hardly proves your point."

Ann's smile is also the smile of one who knows better. But they can't both be right — or can they? By mutual agreement and because the clock on the bank tower shows them it's time, they dispose of their trash, "hug" good-bye, and head in opposite directions toward their respective desks. Petra looks down at her feet, afraid as always of tripping over a cobblestone. Ann watches her retreat as she puts in her earbuds, but something's gone haywire with her music; she won't be able to listen to her favorite diver-timento on the way back. This disturbs her to the point of tears — or is it something else that blurs the path before her? The sun seems higher than it did when she arrived in the park at noon, though she knows this cannot be. She lifts her eyes and squints against it, panicked in momentary blindness before the relief comes again of being able to see.

The children on the playground laugh as she passes, but she decides not to contemplate why.

Why Not Climb?

by David Hawkins

Whether it's a bouldering sheep
or a raw snow-bone,
at this distance all is tantalising
and inconclusive. Either way,

there's a silver flaw in your best eye,
a speck of ore, a day-star.
Your other is flecked with floaters,
brimful with half-formed tears

gelled from the wind.
Either way, whatever *it* is
slides off the precipice
as soon as you shift your gaze.

This guttural rain falls at exactly
45 degrees; your gust-scuppered hood
swells in vacant optimism.
A wet head. A cold head

adrift somewhere between
Magnetic North and True North,
wobbling at the centre
of a tiny antique compass.

Tasseography

by Jacqueline Houton

I don't believe in psychics, but I might owe something to one.

Before my mother was born, my grandmother Jo had her fortune told by a woman who lived in her apartment building. Though I don't know her name, I can picture this woman welcoming Jo into her warm little kitchen, flowing skirt skimming the floor as she poured two cups of tea from the cast-iron kettle. That calm moment amid her neighbor's cozy clutter may have been rare respite for my grandmother, who had a six-year-old son and an eleven-year-old daughter at home. Maybe the steaming vapors loosened something inside her. Maybe she cradled the cup in both hands as she made her confession — that she had been sure her missed periods meant menopause, that she didn't know if she was prepared to become a mother again at her age.

I can see the neighbor staying those hands when my grandmother reached to take her final sip of tea, instructing her to close her eyes and swirl the sediment three times. Jo may have felt a little sheepish, but whether it was curiosity or desperation or some heady brew of both that spurred her on, she did as she was told. Her host smiled into the bottom of the cup, reading my grandmother's fortune in the scattered leaves. She told Jo that she was to give birth to a daughter who would care for her in her old age. And my grandmother did.

My mother has told me a version of this story multiple times, and she must have heard it more than once from her own mother. I always thought it was a good story, but recently my feelings about it have become more complicated. I know it must have been my grandmother's way of saying *I'm so glad I had you.* Maybe it was also her way of expressing the wish that she would be loved and cared for in an uncertain future. Still, I can't imagine ever telling a child she was anything but wanted.

Seventy years after Jo's reading, mysticism is having a moment. Crystals claim space on desktops and nightstands. Astrological signs have become key data points on many online dating profiles. And tarot readers, no longer confined to neon-lit storefronts, interpret beautifully illustrated arcana on Instagram.

Tasseography — the technical term for reading tea leaves — feels downright fusty by comparison. It was the Victorians' favored form of divination, and a democratic one, requiring no special equipment, just the dregs of an everyday drink: a homey and practical magic. The 1921 book *Tea-Cup Reading and Fortune-Telling by Tea Leaves* dubbed it "the simplest, truest, and most easily learned" method, explaining the meanings of myriad symbols, from acorn (improvement in health) to zebra (adventure in foreign lands). Nowadays though, practitioners are far harder to find than tarot readers or palmists or chart-wielding astrologers.

But I found one at a 90-year-old tearoom in New Orleans, a city I'd always wanted to see. I was still bleeding after miscarrying a pregnancy that was emphatically planned. My husband and I had learned that IVF was our only chance for conceiving, and after his-and-hers retrieval surgeries, plus weeks of pills and patches, nightly injections, and early-morning blood-work, we were thrilled to find out I'd gotten pregnant on the first try. But at six and half weeks, the ultrasound heard no heartbeat. I booked tickets a few days later. I'm an anxious flier, but it was winter and I wanted to go someplace warm. I wanted to get out of my body; I could at least get out of New England.

So we walked along the Mississippi River nursing cups of chicory coffee.

We listened to jazz on Frenchmen Street. We ate grilled oysters and drank fizzy cocktails that would have been forbidden a few weeks before. We wandered into voodoo shops crammed with candles, oils, incense, and charms, obeying the do-not-touch signs above altars heaped with offerings of shiny coins and cigarettes. And on our last day, we stumbled upon the tearoom. I'm not sure why I went inside. Though I devoured books about witchcraft and ESP as a kid, I've been a skeptic since adolescence. But I had that scrap of family lore in my head. Maybe I just wanted to hear history rhyme. Maybe I was hoping to get a good story out of it.

My reading was performed by Patricia, who told me to turn my cup seven times, then flip it over. "Let's see what's going on," she said. She told me my lucky number, forecasted career shifts, predicted a trip to the mountains. "I see children," she said. "Do you have children?"

Though I hadn't planned to, I told her I'd had a miscarriage. It may have been the first time I'd actually said the word out loud. I'd informed my PCP through an online patient portal; I'd told the few friends who'd known I was pregnant via text message. Some things are easier to say to a stranger.

This stranger told me that I would have two children, a boy and a girl. And she said that I would be a good mother. I know she was telling me what I wanted to hear, but I still think it was kind. And in that moment it may have been helpful to hear her articulate so matter-of-factly what I hadn't dared hope for out loud.

I hate the idea of hucksters taking money from vulnerable people. I'm wary of woo-woo trends, so quickly co-opted by a capitalist culture that tells us self-care and spirituality are things we can buy. I believe in science and logic and that, in times of trouble, a therapist is a far better person to consult than a fortune teller.

But I also understand a yearning for magic, sometimes a pretty good synonym for a sense of wonder, or a feeling of control. And I believe there is something sad and beautiful about a big-brained animal that sees symbols in random stimuli, that assigns names to arbitrary arrangements of stars, that looks for truth in the bottom of a teacup and meaning in the cards we're dealt. I think it's a minor miracle that we're able to imagine a future when nothing is guaranteed, and no surprise that we sometimes need help getting started again. Tasseography comes from the French *tasse*, meaning "cup," and the Greek *graph*, meaning "writing." We don't read tea leaves; we write stories with them. And stories help us to hope in a world where suffering is easier to predict than joy.

What Grandma Read at the Bottom of My Cup

by Felicia Sanzari Chernesky

The hand that strokes the sleeping cheek will throb
with self-control: a pulsing power station.
Kindness is titanium. So plant.
The seed will burrow up through dirt and time
as air becomes a tempter's kiss and rain
prophetic. Allow these things and life will burst
and course through hand-strewn ashes. Blind river.
What burns grows back, and a promise is a promise,
so why not reap — but only keep what's yours.

The New York Times Publishes 1,000 Names

by Julia Lisella

I don't know about you, but I'm ready for something to be
different. This staying at home, not knowing what's going to
happen next, worrying, not sleeping well... it's tiring.
Email from my yoga teacher, May 26, 2020

Let us be tired

Let us stay and arrange the coffee mugs on a new shelf;
let us stare at the dog;

let us roam around the house forgetting
what we needed to do next. Let us

read the 1000 names knowing they are only
a portion of what ails us —. All morning let's read them.

Let us read the names out loud.
Let us be interested in how the *Times* defines a life and

how we do. How we do. This is the virus and that is the gun.
This is the virus and that is the knee on the neck. This is the
vigil and that is the vigil. This is the breath not taken
and that is the breath not taken. This is the storm and that is the cough.

BY JULIA LISELLA

This is the mask and that is the placard.

Let us hear the fear in a neighbor's cough;
let us hear the fear in a siren.

Let us vigil, let us watch here on our knees, in the sunlight

let us remember to kneel in the sunlight, 8 minutes, 20 minutes, a lifetime

let us reject athletic trainers and yoga teachers and meditation leaders and
        priests and poets.

They mean well. They mean

to get us back into "it"— they are here for "us"

Let us stop feeling relieved if we do not have

underlying conditions. We have underlying conditions.

How I Became Greta and Alan

by Lindsay Coleman

For an absolute stranger, Bob Coyne calls a lot. Over the past two years
or so he has called at least once and sometimes as many as twenty times in
a month. The messages he leaves are gruff and nondescript. "Hi. It's Bob
Coyne. [long, breathy pause]. Call me back. Bye."

The voice is brittle with age, defeated. He knows no one will call him back.
He's ringing into the void.

I am an introvert with trust issues. If a number I don't recognize appears on
my phone, I let it go straight to voicemail. After listening to at least ten of
these cryptic messages over a couple of weeks, I start to get annoyed. I've
been physically assaulted by men who might have voices like his. Who is
this creep? Why is he calling me? What's up with the breathing

After a typical day as a high school teacher of skipping lunch to meet with
students, staying late to coach, and picking up dinner for my family, I stand
in the Whole Foods parking lot and dial Bob's number. The conversation is
terse.

"Hello, this is Lindsay," I explain. "I'm not sure whom you are trying to call,
but I am not that person. You have dialed me consistently every day for the
past two weeks. Please stop calling this number." The phone line clicks and
I don't hear from him for a while.

I block his number when he starts to call again, but for some reason continue to listen to his messages. They're mostly the same. His raspy monotone
reports his name and — as an afterthought — a request to call him back.

Sometimes he hangs up without saying a word.

One time, Bob Coyne calls to say he is trying to get through to the V.A.

One time, Bob Coyne calls and says that he is out of meds.

One time, Bob Coyne calls and says *can you please just call just once. Please.*

A year passes. We are now in the throes of the Covid-19 outbreak. Leadership — from the president, to our city's mayor, to our Secretary of Education — is unraveling. Politics is at war with science. Capitalism shoves people back into unsafe work environments. No one seems to appreciate the precariousness of human life.

Our school is off for the summer and it's anyone's guess what the fall will bring. We all dread the worst, having seen the unfortunate qualities of humankind on display for the last three months. People without masks pack the beaches, declare the virus a hoax, swallow bleach because the president suggests it might be a cure. Nevertheless, in the midst of a pandemic and America's relentless war on science and truth, we are planning to resume business-as-usual at school in the fall.

When Bob Coyne's messages resurface — more frequently — during this time, they feel eerily appropriate: like an agitation in the far reaches of the universe, an anomalous but steady signal from another dimension, a red warning blinking on and off at the end of Midnight Street. *Bob Coyne,* I think. *Please. Go to sleep.*

Eight times. That's how many times Bob Coyne called today. His messages have grown gradually more desperate, like the spool is running out.

In one message, he asks if someone can pick him up some toilet paper. In another, though, he says the name of his daughter, *Greta.* And for the first time something inside me — a wintering outpost from some former era of defense — definitively breaks. I'm not sure what I was afraid of before these times — could I really have been scared of *this?*

When I unblock Bob Coyne's number and call him back, I explain who I am. I am not his daughter, Greta, but I would very much like to help him find her. Is there anyone I could contact to assist in locating her? He politely declines, but actually says my name, along with a "thank you" and "God bless." The sound of my name in his mouth is a kind of reckoning; a glimpse in the mirror after not seeing my reflection for weeks. I'm not sure I like what I see.

He leaves two more messages within five minutes of each other. One is for Greta and Alan, thanking them profusely for their lovely visit that day. But the next one is for me. He says my name again. He says he is sorry he's called so many times. Unfortunately, he admits, he may call again. Again: "Thank you. God bless."

An hour later I have picked up the phone, and he addresses me by name. "How do you know Greta and Alan?" he asks.

I remind him that I don't but that I wish I did. "They sound like lovely people."

Curtly, he agrees that they are. We talk for a little while then. He says he lives in Massachusetts, right down the street from Greta and Alan. Who knows if this is true, but I'd like to think it is, that there is someone close by who knows him. I tell him that I teach outside Philadelphia, but I lived in Boston for a long time, which is how I got this (617) area code.

At the end of this call, we are no closer to finding our way out of the labyrinth. I'm still not sure how, or if I can help him. But there is a light in his voice — something missing from the messages scraping like dead leaves through the last year and a half. He is talking to *me*, which feels like progress, understanding. These conversations might be the last vestiges of a shore on which he once stood with absolute confidence: solid ground we all take for granted. The blankness rolling through Bob's mind is subjective, but its ripples are cosmic. In the eye of that turmoil and chaos, my number is somehow steady, resurfacing between the dips and froth of his consciousness. I actually have no idea what our talks mean to him in the larger context of his life, but I'm beginning to realize what they mean to me.

For six months I have woken up choking with fear, terrorized by dreams of forgetting. Where did I put my keys? Where is my bag? Where did I park the car? Or, my favorite 3 a.m. dream: I'm driving home from school when I realize I forgot my five-year-old daughter at home. Every morning, I take her to school with me where she also attends Pre-K. But in the dream she has been home alone for eleven long hours with no way to contact anyone. Of course, I'm stuck in traffic.

In real life? Days bleed together, as do the online classes that I'm teaching, my daughter's Zoom school, Skype tutoring and meet-ups. My husband has lost his job in the restaurant industry as a result of the pandemic and I've taken on more classes to compensate. My very real ADHD — coupled with the constant change and interruption of schedules and news updates — is like getting hit, wave after wave, without any chance to recover. Friends appear and disappear from computer screens, and I wake up each morning trying desperately to remember what happened the day before, what was real and what was a dream and — if it matters — what basic tasks I need to complete that day. I know I'm not alone. We are all drowning.

On the phone, I want to whisper into the windy hollows of the receiving side: *Bob, thank God you called. I can't tell what's real anymore, but it doesn't matter. I actually don't care about any of it. Not the dream, not the waking nightmare. I don't see the validity or value of any of it, Bob. I love my daughter and my husband beyond measure, but you see it doesn't matter. It isn't enough. Without the illusion of progress that kept us busy all of these stupid years, what's left?*

When Bob Coyne finally finds me and I make the adult decision to unblock his calls and talk to him — knowing it may lead nowhere and may do nothing practically to solve the "problem"— I wonder if maybe I'm not, in a way, kind of like Greta and Alan: questionably real, imaginatively relevant, trying to live up to an ideal or an idea that I'll admit is just as lifesaving for me as it might be for Bob. In another life, I'd like to believe that I did this from the beginning: that I'd opened the lines of communication for someone more genuine and vulnerable than myself. I wish I had that capacity for humanness in me. Then, I would have been here the whole time on this only, very real and disappearing shoreline.

As shuddering as reality is these days, I want to think that there is a way that one lost soul can knock on a door, and keep knocking until the person on the other side — numb, estranged, adrift — finally hears a heart.

IN HEAT

By ANGIE KANG

We had severely
misjudged the sun.
By the time we got
home, the damage had
already been done.

So we sprung
to action.

We slept with the fan
on and tried to interlock
our sticky legs, but our
bodies tore in reluctant
separation.

"Ow," you said.
"Ow," I agreed.

We settled for holding
hands and sometime in
the night let go of the
other's soft palms.

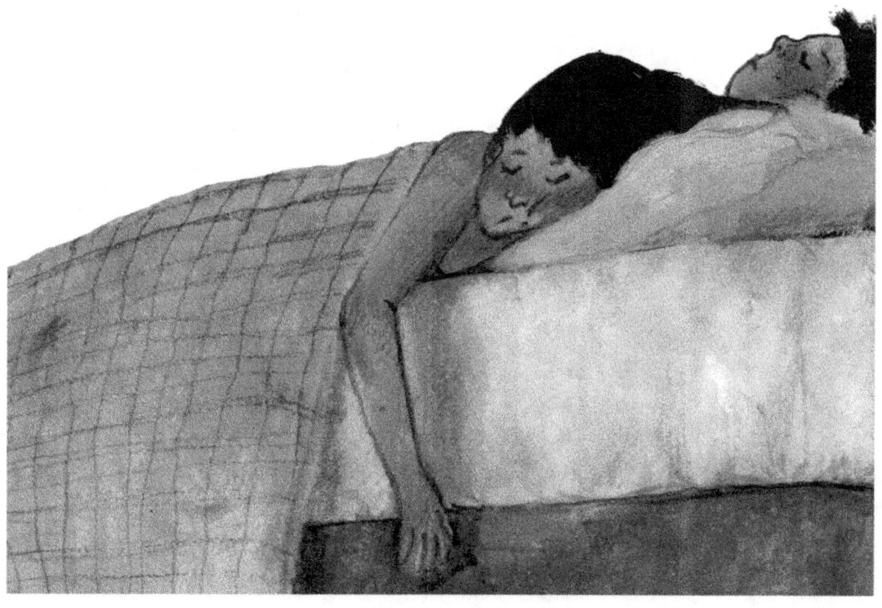

In the morning,
we took a shower
together and let the
icy streams baptize
us awake.

I wrapped my arms
around you and
we stood there
just like that, wet
and dripping and
radiating heat.

We gave ourselves
up to that heat:

Welcomed
it inside,

steeped our
joys in it,

found comfort in
its embrace.

After a few days,
when the peeling
started, we embraced
that too.

Bit by bit, we peeled
ourselves clean of
defenses.

We bid farewell to
layers and layers
of our past selves,

and when the time came
that our skin had stopped
flaking entirely,

we looked at the
dusty pile of what
we once were,

and then turned
to each other
to see what we
had become.

Aspiration

by Allison A. deFreese

Crowned
a week before
Easter.
It is spring.
The spirit
might have whispered
in your ear,
as with Mary;
the virus
could have entered
though the eye,
through other openings.

Your uvula once pink
and light as paperwhites,
as cloudless sulfur—
tightening in flame
the world ablaze.

Your throat
a ghost ship
docked dry
before floating
a forty day
quarantine
on the long tail

into the nebula
of lungs,
or sponge
turned to coral.

The bronchi,
a tree inverted,
braying as you
take root
in pluvial waters
rising, air hungry
alveoli.

Spikes on the cross
atop the monde
on a diadem.
It is spring — hail,
the rain lands heavy
everywhere.
The world inside.
Will you drown
while waiting to fly
to save time,
another life
to aspire to something?
Gazing skyward from bed,
connected and vented —
instead you take
another breath.

The School of Working Women: A Letter to My Mother

by Katie Taylor

Dear Mom,

Greetings from Seattle. It's going on ten months without seeing you, but I swear I hear and smell you in the pre-lucid hours of morning. Pot lids clattering to the linoleum to make way for the Crock-Pot from the back of the cabinet. A knife slapping the cutting board, slicing through onion or potato. The Conair curling iron heating-up on the bathroom vanity that emits an aroma of thrice-baked Rave ExtraHold. The dryer dial cranking to a halt, signaling the drum to start its spin. You calling to me from my bedroom doorway — smartly dressed in last season's Talbots, hair coiffed à la Diana, smelling like honeysuckle, and ready for "real" work — wakes me from my dream. You're not here, you're in Tennessee. And the year isn't 1989, it's 2021.

I've been having these dreams for good reason. Being a mother and teacher during this pandemic eerily mirrors memories of you, and other moms in the Eighties, raising the kids as you labored, sometimes paid, mostly under or unpaid. Reflecting on you and my *othermothers*, women simultaneously working and caregiving feels less like an anomaly during this public health crisis and more of a return to the historical workday. But a major difference between you and me-as-Mom is that my partner works and takes care of others by my side; your grandchildren see your son-in-law's work in all its forms.

As I remember it, Dad worked at work and recreated at home. I knew Dad worked at the aluminum company in town, that Beth's dad was a lawyer, and Jessica's was a postman. Yet I had no access to these jobs, never went to their offices, nor knew really anything about the day-to-day operations of their professions. My observations of these men were of them seated in front of Braves games on TV, scooping forkfuls of mashed potatoes or beans at the dinner table, or sometimes fiddling around the yard, rake in hand. I only heard about their jobs in passing comments from you, the wives.

"Dad's working the night shift."
"Jim has a new client."
"Doug has to be at his truck by 4am."

But ask me about *your* work, Beth's mom's work, and Jessica's mom's work? Well, that is a different story.

You cared for us kids *while* at work, and worked as caregivers without stop. I knew you helped elementary school children learn to read and do math. From a nearby desk, peering across the top of my *Babysitter's Club* book, I watched you lean in to students to pass along gentle guidance and encouragement. Beth's mom had her own classroom of first graders. I heard about her anxieties for students as she decompressed in the car, taking me and Beth to ballet lessons, or in conversations I overheard with you. Jessica's mom (wo)manned the main office at my middle school. As Jessica and I snacked on cheese crackers and cans of Fresca she saved for us from the lunch she never had time to eat, I watched her type and patiently answer parents' in-person questions from our "secret" perch behind her desk chair.

Mom, I attended the School of Working Women: a front row seat to women taking care of other people's children while taking care of their own. Women waking-up at ungodly hours to make themselves look presentable for a long day of interfacing with others. Women putting the kids to bed at a reasonable time, just to do another work shift of cleaning dishes, doing loads of laundry, and paying bills. Women working together to make a school day — a school*house* — hum along, to keep the kids fed, to ensure no one missed a lesson. Women changing-up the routine when a child got sick or transitioned to a different classroom, or when the holiday season crammed the calendar with rehearsals and potlucks. Women collaboratively piecing together supervision and carpools in lieu of free after-school care and public transit absent in most small towns. Women making a lot less money than their husbands but seemingly doing all the work.

I have a theory. My own sex and gender-inflected interests inherently clouded my view on men's work. Had I been more into sports, perhaps I would have seen men coaching, lugging bags of soccer balls and coolers from truck beds. Had Dad owned his own business, perhaps I would have hung by his desk chair after school, watching him keep the books or thoughtfully troubleshoot personnel issues. But as it was, children were not permitted behind company lines. We weren't allowed to tag along to trial. We couldn't ride in the back of the USPS truck. If such a time ever arose, it was a token "Bring Your Daughter to Work Day." Those work parodies were followed by one of you moms picking us up to take us back to work with you.

Remember when I went away to the Big City for college? A universe of potential career trajectories opened-up before me. Yet when I imagined myself doing work, all I could envision was caring for children. Is this a coincidence? Assuredly, no. Caregiving as work is what I knew, having seen it modeled by you and other moms. I majored in urban studies, focusing on the urban education strand. I interned at shelters housing women and their children. Beth and I worked as counselors at an all-girls summer camp in North Carolina. I taught English to Japanese high school students. I mentored homeless youth in a residential program in Nashville. I taught Social

Studies at an alternative high school. I studied youth development in graduate school. As you know, Beth became an elementary school teacher and Jessica runs her own online sewing shop, specializing in children's clothes.

Now that the pandemic forces me to teach college students from my home computer, your two grandchildren are next to *me* while I work. They watch me respond to student emails during Zoom breaks. They hear me decompress with my women colleagues over the uncertainty of graduate student funding and the aching loneliness undergraduates express in their online assignments. As they snack on yogurt and chips held back from the lunch I never had time to eat, my boys shyly respond to co-workers' questions about their school days spent in our impromptu schoolhouse. They, too, attend the School of Working Women. Now I understand that you, Beth's mom, and Jessica's mom loved us but didn't love managing us while doing your paid labor. At best, working two jobs at once means feeling like you're doing neither particularly well. At worst, it means always being on the verge of losing your mind. In these moments, and with nowhere to go because of the pandemic, I find some sense of relief (or is it productivity?) slicing onions or potatoes, experimenting with a new ponytail style, or starting a load of bath towels.

At the beginning of this crisis, I hoped the pandemic would break the cycle, that dads also working from home would be an adequate substitute for direct observation of a "profession" for the kids. With men caregiving too, will society finally take Angela Davis's argument to heart and start compensating domestic labor? But one year in, the hours my partner spends in-person at his lab tick-up while I continue working from home. The news of women dropping out of their chosen professions to focus on home-work makes me see little has changed.

Years later and miles removed from me, you, Beth's mother, and Jessica's mother continue to labor unpaid; you take care of your infirm husbands.

These men, beaten down by years of paid work and unschooled in domestic tasks, rely almost entirely on you, the wives, for daily survival. None of the chauffeuring, cooking, scheduling, feeding, cleaning, and coordinating with other women has ceased for you. If you had been adequately compensated for being an educator and for all those hours of domestic labor over fifty years of marriage, you could make a choice today: continue caregiving or pay for help and have a much deserved break.

The work-home changes wrought by the pandemic make me want to quit something, *just one thing*, everyday. But more broadly, it has unveiled the tenuous separation between paid and unpaid work many women of your generation struggled to gain for my generation but never got to enjoy. My generation of mothers, sisters, daughters, and aunties reaped the rewards of your labor, at least until this pandemic came along. Now once again — as if we never left the Eighties — we knit a patchwork of local, benevolent support in the absence of universal childcare and healthcare and standardized maternity leave. Before schools, offices, and laboratories reopen to those of us working from home, all caregivers, women and men, need a plan for the next crisis, and the next. Otherwise, we mothers will, once again, fill in the gaps left by the absence of policies for families to survive. So, Mom, in this new year, like you, I'll keep working and caregiving, because that's what mothers do.

Your loving daughter

Missing

by SM Stubbs

Late spring, nights still cold, the stars clear
as spotlights, people I love keep dying.
Every week a different shocking loss:
cancer, gunshot, embolism, suicide, on and on.

These sudden gaps leave me
feeling like my mom did after her stroke:
when the neurologist asked her to identify people
in photos she could name only those

on the starboard half. She'd stare, silent,
confounded by who we swore she'd missed.
Later, when asked to fill a blank clock,
she packed 1 through 12 onto the right side.

They say the earth's 71% water, the body 60%, that
we share the tides' highs and lows.
If anyone dies today they'll be kelp and fish
while I do dishes, check daily lists.

I sink to the bottom of the ocean
in my dreams. I cross trenches of primordial mud
filled with lives I can't pronounce.
Asleep, I'm certain the deceased come back

as deep-sea creatures, pale and blinded
by sunlight. At these depths none of us are dead or
we all are, and together we sway
at the mercy of the moon.

Pocha

by Janet Rodriguez

My friend, Leticia, is in the middle of telling me a funny story in the Spanglish we often speak together. We're on an escalator and she's trying to keep her voice down, but she's half-laughing and it's hard for her to control her volume when she's like this.

"Y mi nieto dice, 'Abuela, why are you….'" Leticia laughs into her fist and squeezes her legs together. It takes a few seconds for her to say the rest of what her grandson said: "¿Por qué lleva un pañal?"

Then, she looks at me. For a moment, I feel stupid. Uncool. Lost. I'm floundering…trying to retrieve the word: Un pañal…un pañal….what is un pañal? Instead of asking, I pretend to understand. I laugh until we reach the top of the escalator and step off. She looks at me again. I wonder if she can tell I'm an idiot, a faker, a fraud. A pocha.

"He asked me why I was wearing a diaper," she tells me. "A diaper! My panty lines were so noticeable he thought I was wearing a diaper!"

"How embarrassing," I say. I mean it.

***

I'm embarrassed to admit it, but there's not enough Spanish in my brain. My Mexican-American mother speaks the language fluently, but my siblings and I don't because:

1. My father is Irish-American. He always spoke English to her and us —

just like the world around us.

2. I grew up in a cowtown in the middle of California, where English surrounded us on all sides. There was almost no opportunity to use the language, since everyone was speaking English.

3. In the 1970s, speaking Spanish was still discouraged in schools, unless you were in Spanish class. Even so, curriculum included phrases, like ¿Donde está la biblioteca?

4. I have a problem memorizing the oceans of irregular verbs and verb tenses.

Pick a reason why I don't speak fluent Spanish; there are so many to choose from. I have a closet of excuses in all different shapes and sizes. There is one reason I rarely examine: Spanish was systematically stolen from me. My inheritance, la lengua de mi corozon y mis antepasados, was taken from me before I was born. A widespread belief, a value system that infiltrated the educational system, decided for me that Americans should speak *only* English.

One generation before me, children of immigrants were made to feel ashamed for speaking Spanish. They subsequently raised children to speak perfect English. My generation feels shame for not speaking Spanish, even when our names or complexions suggest that we should. Somewhere along the line, mi lengua was removed from my quiver and I'm not empty-handed. No one is taking responsibility for this theft. I'm slighted out of my inheritance.

Today most people living in the United States recognize the need for fluency in at least one other language. I watched a TED talk where a polyglot — someone who speaks more than three languages — proclaimed that there is no secret to learning languages, you just have to do it. I wanted to leave a rude comment, telling her she's clueless, but I didn't. Instead, I drift off, and remember how the subject of Spanish is barbed, like wire. Even Grandma knew it was the language of the oppressor, the empirical Spaniards, who conquered a conquerable people and robbed my poor ancestors of their land. The Spaniards enslaved them, had them plant and harvest sugar, then sold it to the rest of the world. An underpaid and underfed workforce, many Mexican people starved.

Oddly enough, the Spanish language became the replacement language for the indigenous people when they surrendered their own. A widespread belief, a value system that infiltrated the educational system, decided for them that Mexicans should speak *only* Spanish.

And yet, Spanish is the only thing that connects me to my grandparents' homeland. I remember them speaking it, and I want it in my life. It's the only thing that I can't seem to conquer, no matter how hard I try. While I was thinking this, I accidentally heard something the polyglot said: Take the learning into your own hands.

She's right. The only way for me to repatriate mi lengua is with my own clumsy hands. I try a little every day, like a child building a bridge out of popsicle sticks. I join a Spanish speaking writers' group. My fellow writers switch back and forth, from English to Spanish, accomplished as swordfighters. My first attempts at writing and reading my work in Español are raw and painful. My fellow writers squirm as I try to pronounce some words, but they don't laugh. They accept me and my insane mission. They encourage me to keep trying, but accept myself as I am.

When my mom hears my Spanish poetry, she corrects my pronunciation in some places. When I'm finished, she smiles. She tells me I've made a good effort, but adds that I should stick to writing poetry in my own language. I don't know how to answer.

A few days after she hears me read this essay aloud, one of my new friends from my writers' group offers to teach me Spanish. She does this for free, during this pandemic. Learning Spanish on her front porch has proven to be harder than I imagined, especially memorizing so many nouns. Human beings love naming everything in the universe, seen and unseen. Memorizing nouns is critical if you want to describe a complicated world. Some nouns are purposefully cruel. The worst one is *pocha*: a Mexican-American woman who can't speak Spanish.

I vow to overcome this noun, even if it takes me a lifetime.

Alone

by Jonathan Andrew Pérez

From childhood, on Pitkin and Easton Avenue, I have not been
As others were: I have not seen —
Portals eclipsed by the clamor of the boulevard, a wet season brings
In and washes all who lie *Face Down Hands Up*. No common spring
But a dog barking, and brushfoot nymphalid butterflies left untaken
From the cracks in Brownsville's streets. What carried what awakened
In the ground-dirt, where *Face Down Hands Up*, at the same tone
Performs the sunlight, performs the 15 police car *Burletta per musica* — I alone —
Then, in unconscious crescendo, the unison of municipal trees, in the dawn
The stormy night heaved the yellow-taped lines, the lifeless chalk-drawn
Scratching every depth of a family noted and quickly eating brunch to ID, ill
From portals of new seasons of violence, the pastoral remains still
In me — without being overly-performative binds in me still
From the torrent of mass policing, the torrent of Right(eous), a fountain
Like urgency, like the migration of brushfoot butterflies, up mountains
From West Virginia North to Brownsville, Brooklyn, and rolled
Around the sunlight, swerved with never-ending crime, a gold
Like a tint on a Chevrolet passing the local playground, lighting up inside the sky,
As all passes me by, where is the music, where is the sign, *Face Down Hands Up*
And the cloud that took the form of a dry season —
Sensually teases us like Heaven (if ever blue)
There is a demon in full view –

I rise and put my hands down and stand up. Bathed by new pre-torrential light.

My First Reading,
St. Mark's Poetry Project 1975

by Patricia Spears Jones

I gave my first major public poetry reading in June 1975. It was the St. Mark's Poetry Project annual workshop reading. All of the people who attended the workshops had a chance to perform. Prior to that reading, I had a huge bout of stage fright. I had gone to the Broome Street Bar in SoHo a couple of hours before the event and became so anxious, I left the restaurant. I walked to the traffic island on Broome Street and sat there until I could calm down and then take the subway up to Astor Place to get to St. Mark's Church and read. It was a funny way to celebrate a year of learning to be a poet.

Starting in 1974, I attended a range of free workshops at St. Mark's Church. The Church was a kind of oasis in the midst of crumbling buildings and oddly successful institutions — catty corner from it was the Second Avenue Delicatessen. Father Ortega, the parish priest, encouraged a range of cultural and community projects as he saw the economic stress and the civic neglect that marked the East Village. There, many wonderful shops thrived — the variety store down the block on Second Avenue; a store on E. 9th Street and 2nd Avenue that sold beautiful dresses from the 1940s and 50s. I bought a 1940s dark green dress with a sweetheart décolletage and swag. I was learning to seriously embrace my feminine side, plus it was $10! With silver platform heels, I was ready to sashay my stuff just about anywhere. The store Back from Guatemala on E. 6th Street and St. Mark's Bookstore on St. Mark's Place offered up braided bags and colorful scarves off the "hippie trail." I discovered concert spaces, jazz clubs, and restaurants that sold food that looked familiar, but tasted different: dumplings at Veselka were called pierogis. It seems that I thrive in Gothic piles — my college campus looked like Yale or Princeton — and St. Mark's Church, which still had its pews and altar and was one of the oldest churches in the entire city, was just such a Gothic space. Much that was new took place within those heavy stone walls.

Charlotte Carter, the only other Black person I consistently saw at the Project in the early seventies, is an amazing writer. Even then she seemed to have mastered the prose poem, but as I realized with writers, she wanted to learn more, challenge herself, and see what others were doing. She was taking Bernadette Mayer's workshop that focused on dreams. I joined the workshop. This proved my downfall. I am a light sleeper — I rarely have dreams. So the idea of writing out my dreams was out of the question. Damn. I peeped into Ted Berrigan's workshop and it felt like I was in school with all of the folks who were stoned or drunk and he was orchestrating the chaos. Many talented people in the workshop, but all that booze and grass. Too much.

So, Lewis Warsh, whose workshop I took first, was the one I stayed with and to this day I am grateful. Lewis, who grew up in New York City and who had already published a few collections and started Angel Hair Press with his former wife Anne Waldman, was skinny and handsome with long hair and that sort of laidback sexiness that seems essential to Scorpios. He had a way of focusing on a word, phrase, or line and sort of teasing out what should or should not be there. This could be blunt or very subtle. I don't remember him ever saying something was crap (I did hear that in other workshops), but the weaker or disinterested writers slowly left the workshop leaving a band of very smart, imaginative people in their wake.

Lewis looked at my lyrics and, well, between him and everyone else, the adolescence in my writing departed. In a way, what was happening in the workshop was what was happening to me. I would bring in these long shifting pieces. Lewis would look at them and say, "What's really going on?" And then I would see what was really going on. So would everyone else. The workshop was lively.

My fellow disciples included Bill Kushner who was a playwright and gay, but until the workshop had not quite embraced his queerness in his poetry. He was our cheerleader and he and Guy had the best battles royale. Guy Gauthier would declare, "EVERYTHING IS POETRY!" And I would say, "Really, like everything?" And then we would have this discussion about what was and was not poetry. It could get funny. One time somebody brought a tomato and said, "Is that a poem?" And Guy declared, "Yes!" We laughed a great deal in that workshop.

Robin Messing, born and bred in Brooklyn, was pretty and smart and soft spoken, but we quickly realized that soft spoken was not "push over" — her work was powerful. Yuki Hartman, a Japanese-American poet, experimented with form, especially prose poems and often wrote five poems to everyone else's one. Maggie Staiger aka Maggie Dubris was in a rock-and-roll band (not a punk band, a rock band) and the actor Richard Edson came and went, but when he showed up brought a sense of comedy to the room. Dom Sotelo, whose unexpected death cast a pall over us, was decidedly melancholy. And Diane Raintree was utterly sophisticated. We came into the Parish Hall with our typed sheets of paper and our desire to make work that moved as swiftly or as slowly as the city moved.

Because the city could be slow — could stick you in a puddle of distraction. The book stalls outside the Strand; the store fronts where someone's obsession — toy soldiers, Judaica, vintage dresses — were displayed for eventual sale. The city could make you lurch like the junkies on E. 10th Street or it could swiftly slap you down. One day I was walking with two of my White male friends visiting from the South and this Black guy tried to burn me with a cigarette. One day I went to a rental on E. 5th Street and the White woman slammed the door in my face. Or the city could lift me: I can still see this Black skateboarder navigating Lafayette, no trucks, cars, buses in sight — he seemed to have found some deep bliss and I got to watch him fly. And the relentless catcalls from men: White, Black, Puerto Rican, et al made me and many women card-carrying feminists.

I look at that slender young woman with an Afro bloom of hair on her head and huge eyeglass frames in the picture on the cover of *8:30,* our workshop publication and think, what she was hiding? For I was hiding a deep fear that where I was and what I was doing was a matter of luck and nerve and that at any moment, it would all fall apart.

The Workshop helped me to begin thinking differently about my own creativity, my sense of self. A teasing comment from Bill Kushner or a gentle critique from Robin or Lewis's incisiveness with someone else's work and I could see what was working, where the music was in the line. The Poetry Project hummed and hissed and howled with our attempts to make and remake poetry and our poems and to claim adulthood. I became a poet who could write in the second stanza of a poem entitled "Trees":

There's a tree in the yard
Of my home in Arkansas
I don't know its name
The leaves are pointed
The trunk is thin
It's a great tree to climb
When you're a child
It isn't strong enough
For adolescents or adults
I climbed it once after
Getting my hair done

My mama caught me
And gave me a whipping
It was the last whipping
I got
That was the last tree
I climbed.

I know that my workshop colleagues urged me to make that poem which started out sort of quasi Nikki Giovanni into something more personal — they urged me to trust my own experience in poems. I could use racial markers and show family conflict without it seeming like a huge problem. We were all learning to shed our adolescent thinking and to become the poets that we needed to be. It was a place of great trust and generosity.

But the Poetry Project was not always a place of trust or generosity. While Anne Waldman and Bernadette Mayer were serious poets and organizers and Maureen Owen was producing great issues of *Telephone*, etc., it was a place created and defined by White male poets, some of whom were helpful, others sexually predatory or dismissive. And to be young, gifted, pretty and Black was an anomaly. To be young, gifted, Black and female was to become a feminist. My workshop colleagues knew me, cared about me, watched out for me. But others did not. Journals published poets, esp. the ones who were in Berrigan's workshop; anthologies included everyone but Charlotte and me. I fought against ongoing erasure by working with colleagues on their journals and writing literary reviews in the *Poetry Project Newsletter*. I insisted on a byline. The struggle for visibility had begun. I edited and published *WB*, a mimeo literary magazine, but could not raise funds to make a second issue.

It took working with women poets from other parts of the East Village, especially on organizing readings, that led me to meeting June Jordan and Audre Lorde and Marilyn Hacker. They were involved with Woman

Books on the Upper West Side and Djuna Books in Greenwich Village. And as these connections were happening, I started to go hear music, the "Loft Jazz" scene was starting to erupt. Eventually, three years later, many of we young women poets made our mark with *Ordinary Women*, which I co-edited with Sara Miles, Fay Chiang and Sandra Maria Esteves for which Adrienne Rich wrote the introduction — the first multicultural, multiracial women's poetry anthology on the East Coast.

But in 1975, I realized that ambition was not a bad word. That first workshop gave me that understanding. The Poetry Project workshop provided what a great space of learning has to, a place to meet with writers I respected and came to love. I was a trusted colleague, a good friend, a go-to-person, who was willing to learn how to stand up as a grown up, Afro-bloomed with a sense of encouragement, some hope, and the ability to stand in the nave at St. Mark's Church on a warm June night and read my new poems with confidence; voice still too soft, but soon it would get louder.

Short History of the Accident

by Judith Skillman

Each morning the same skull fracture, an indented line I trace with my fingers in the shower while washing my hair.

The drunk leaning over, telling me it would be OK as I screamed my son's name.

His flannel shirt and his breath to which I return decades later.

This intention, reader, to procrastinate against pain — we share that — knowing all that must be gotten through in the palimpsests of age.

No rain, clear night, 7 pm, a two-year-old's Lego motorcycle lands upside down beside a drain in the five-lane street.

Rushed to settlement, told it was my fault on account of the boot.

Told jay walking.

For the sake of amnesia I bend again to pick up the boot one size too large caring only whether or not this little story about my son remains alive.

Flower Eyes

by Rhiannon McCarthy

The goat was the tricky bit.

The bath had been easy. Her maid hadn't even thought the request strange.

"The mistress were only brush and petals last May Day," the maid had said to the cook. "What's a bath by the river in the autumn chill to a creature made of hawthorne and chestnut?"

The fishnet was no harder, really. She'd only needed her eyelashes. The men by the boats were always so happy to help once they saw her eyelashes.

The spearhead had given her slightly more pause. Bit of a scheduling nightmare that one, really. Missing mass for a full year would have been noticed by the ladies who kept the altar dusted and swept, if no one else, and they would talk. She'd had to get help and take it in turns—her and her lover. They'd traded off Sundays—taking to bed every other week with some illness—sometimes twice in a row, just to keep the tale alive and believable.

The babe helped, too. Her husband was eager for a son to sit on his throne, so it was easy enough to plead the babe and take to her bed, guarding that precious cargo he'd wedged between her legs. He never knew she spent those days at the forge instead, pounding bronze to a sharp, fine edge, fit to slice through rib and muscle and set her free.

So it took some doing, but she had the spear and the bath and the net and the riverside, and now she was fighting with the damn goat, because it, at least, did not give a damn about her eyelashes or her newly heavy breasts —

swelled with new milk now her daughter was born — or her tiny waist or her dainty ankles, or any other part of her frankly ridiculous form that so many men went absolutely witless for.

They'd made her this way — a weapon that was the sum of all desire. Crafted her from stick and cloth and flower and given her flesh. Flesh tailored to their own lust — her husband and his creeping uncle. They'd made her as a gift for themselves. A piece of the land they could conquer and own. They'd given her towering hills and soft, smooth valleys — curves to rival the rolling pastures and skin as bright as the primrose petal — and all this in aid of a throne and a son who'd been a cursed daughter instead.

But before the birth, he'd loved her. Her husband. He'd loved the idea of her, anyway. The reflection of his desire in her living body. He'd been so eager to please — so happy to tell her how clever he'd been. How he could only be killed by a river while trapped in a net and struck by a spear forged for a year while everyone else attended mass, with one foot in a bath and one foot on a stubborn, impossible, pigheaded black goat.

It was bad enough that it had to be black. Completely black — from head to hoof. She'd spent the last months of her pregnancy visiting farms all over the kingdom, looking for one goat without a spot of white in its coat. Her husband thought she was finally taking an interest in being Queen. Her people thought she had a fetish for livestock. They'd finally just started bringing black goats to her — a parade of them through the great hall that would have been extremely suspicious if her husband was ever home. He wasn't, even for the birth. The right goat had arrived the next day.

It had arrived just in time, but the goat wouldn't be moved now. The farmer had tied it up to a tree down by the river for her — blushing and muttering about witches and royals and the proclivities thereof — but even after she untied the goat, it wouldn't budge. Her lover was supposed to be here. Maybe he could have led the goat, but he'd taken fright and run in the night. He wasn't made of oak and nettle — not like her. He wasn't made of much of anything — just dreams and wishing. Dreams that were gone now like everything else but the damn goat, which just sat before her and stared with dark, dull eyes, chewing bark. Blissfully unaware of her husband — finally home and easily persuaded to bathe before seeing his disappointment of a daughter — who was sitting in his bath by the river in the next copse of trees, nearly ready to get out.

She looked at the goat with its calm, dead eyes, and she envied it. That it could sit here in the wood and not be moved by force, or beauty, or love. How peaceful it must be, to sit and eat and not give a damn about where you came from and who brought you here and where they were going to drag you to next. The goat would not be dragged. The goat would not be born and wed and bred all on the same day, all without its consent. The goat would not go to the bath unless it pleased, and it did not please. It did not please at all.

The net would never be cast now. The spear would never be thrown. The bath by the river would only make her husband smell all the sweeter when he came to her tonight to start on the son she owed him.

She wept then — sunk to her knees on the forest floor, struggling to stifle soft, broken sounds that might alert her husband nearby. She hadn't cried since they'd made her. Flowers don't cry when you crush them — they curl up and shrivel instead. She had. She'd been born with all the joy of the forest and the fields at sunrise; she'd been wedded and bedded before sunset. And something inside her had shrunk — pulled away from the insides. Something vital and delicate and small. It had curled up and laid down, ready to die.

But she couldn't die. She bled water, not blood. She was a flower — and a flower has no wrists to slit. She couldn't leave, so her husband would have to go instead, and he would have, if it hadn't been for the damn goat.

It was licking her face now. Lapping up tears. It should have been sickening, but she was beyond caring now. What part of her hadn't been touched by worse? Pawing hands and searching eyes. Pounding, hammering flesh. The goat was practically an improvement. Her laugh was harsh and bright — choked back before the sound could carry too far. Maybe the farmers were right. Maybe livestock had more to offer than men.

Eventually, she ran out of water for tears. The goat still watched her with dull, dark eyes. Unbothered. She leaned in close and gave it a kiss on the head — right between the horns.

"Sorry," she said, muffled by the dark, musty hair on its crown. "I know what it is to be led."

She stood then and collected her things — the net she'd bought with her beauty and the spear she'd forged with her rage. She turned once more to the goat and bowed.

"Go," she said. "Find your way to greener fields, my friend."

The goat said nothing — just sat there and stared. Actually, she was lucky. It could have bleated and made a racket, and then her husband would rush out of the bath and find her here with all the ingredients for his death. Maybe that would be a blessing? Surely he wouldn't keep a would-be assassin for his Queen? Maybe they'd let her become flowers again. Let her blow to seed. Let her fly in the wind — finally, finally free.

But the goat didn't bleat. It didn't make a sound. It winked, and it turned, and it trotted to the river and the copse of trees where her husband's bath must finally be turning cold.

She watched it go — heading right where she needed it to be — and then she shook herself and ran, net and spear in hand.

She could hear her husband splashing and singing old songs about women won in battle. The goat stalked him through the trees — a hunter after deadly prey. Her husband's back was gooseflesh in the chill air — broad and damp and clean. A warrior — beautifully made — all muscle and dark curls. She might have found him handsome, once, if he'd ever given her the chance.

He never saw the goat. He stood and the water ran — down round buttocks and powerful thighs, well turned calves and strong feet — one planted in the bath and one rising — suspended — over the back of the goat.

It landed and so did her net. He fought like a wild thing, but his fishermen knew their business, and the net held while she hefted the spear and heaved.

She was aiming for his heart, but the spear was heavy, and she missed. It pierced his ass instead. It traveled through and through.

He died. It took long enough. Long enough for him to see her there, kneeling beside him with the goat, who was bleating softly now and chewing on the drying cloth that would never be needed again. The goat looked content, and so was she. Even her husband looked peaceful, somehow. Like loving her against her will had been a prison for him, too. They were both free now, one way or another.

His uncle found her first. She could have run, of course, but there didn't seem to be much point, now. Her daughter was in the castle, and her lover was probably halfway to the mountains, and her husband was dead. Her work was done.

Her uncle-in-law banished the goat. He tried to kill it, but even his magic couldn't spell a blade to cut through its pitch black coat, and she was glad when the old wizard finally gave up and told the goat to go. The goat left immediately. It didn't look back.

The wizard didn't unmake her. She was ready for it, but something stayed his hand. He had built her, after all — of stick and cloth and all the flowers he could find. He'd spent weeks crafting her to be everything he could imagine his nephew would love, and perhaps he loved her, too. Perhaps creation comes with its own cost. He'd made her to be perfectly obedient in every way, but he'd given her a spark of his life as well. A sense of self that grew in her until the narrow borders of her existence became unbearable, as he would have found them unbearable. Maybe he looked into her eyes and saw himself and all his dreams that would never be.

So he spared her life, but she couldn't stay. They both knew that. He had her bound and brought to the castle gate, so all within could see her banished. They poured out into the darkening hills — servants and warriors and lords. The nursemaid came with the babe — her daughter. She'd never known who fathered the girl — her husband or her lover. It didn't much matter. The babe was hers, and they would hate her for it.

They all clustered around the wizard. He was speaking of grief and treachery and punishment. She was listening to the wood at her back — hoots and squeaks and wind in the trees. The rustle of life that would go on without her.

Or with her, as the case may be. The wizard turned her into an owl — with feathers like petals around her big eyes and creamy white plumage like rowan flowers. She was beautiful still and always. She was all he thought she should be.

He told the crowd this form would be the greatest punishment for her. She was born from flowers who drink in the sun, and as an owl she would never see it again.

The crowd wasn't listening. They were distracted by the nursemaid, who had finally noticed that the babe in her arms was no longer a babe at all but an owlet — white and fluffy and squawking through a beak that was entirely too close to her nipples for comfort. She dropped the owlet with a scream, and it went. Over the crowd. Over the wizard. Over the brush at the start of the wood and into the trees.

Her mother watched her go with new night eyes. She was something precious and free and hers. The moon was bright — so much brighter than the sun had ever been. She beat her wings —

And flew.

I Develop a Crush on My Psychiatrist

by Dani Janae

And here she is: thirst.
A parable about a drowning
man. A skull found by the edge
of a river. Gully of a mouth,

bank of a woman. What can
be filled with bird song alone?
The body craves. Contact. Salt
living like an eel on my tongue.

Whereas the pills are a chart
of little stars. Whereas chemistry
is a love song between two wards.
Whereas she told me: "you will

become more of who you are."
Her name a net in which we
catch my self. The diagnosis
thumbs the pages of my spine:

a diagram of want marked
here. A warning. A prophecy
on brittleness. A fable on
the origins of heat

humming in commune
with my blood the skull,
its mouth cracked
open, miming "feed."

Robot in the Closet

by Shana R. Ashar

The night of the first expulsion, I asked the robot in my closet what to do. Usually when I asked him a question about the meaning of life, the universe and everything, he'd respond with something funny like "reply hazy try again" or "all your base are belong to us" or just "42." He knew what I liked. This time, he paused, made a sound like swallowing, and said, his voice flat and almost human:

"Every scenario I compute ends in chaos."

There was no need to ask him what he meant. I, too, had been monitoring the signs, assembling my own equations. The expulsions had been forecast since the beginning of the regime, and, now, "the removal of the undesirables from our great nation" was finally coming to pass. Back when the regime first took power, Gerry had been here, his shoes lined up neatly outside the door and the smell of his cologne wafting out of the bathroom. Then, we were just two men who shared an apartment and might get married someday. We spent our days at the office, our evenings cooking elaborate meals and holding hands on our couch watching HBO. In bed, he'd curl up next to me, put his head on my chest, and I'd touch his hair until he slept, listening to him breathe.

The work camps came first. Gerry being what he was and us being a secret, he got called to go. He was a high-level computer guy – exactly what they needed. They gave him this lanyard to wear around his neck, attached to a laminated photo ID card with his real name, Ghazir, and an asterisk to mark him. He looked like himself in the photo, all wild hair and eyes full of hope, his shoulders sagging in a way I knew only I could see.

The workers, it seemed, had so much to do that the regime had them move in a few months later. On our last night together, I helped Gerry pack his things into the giant suitcase his dad had brought from India forty years earlier. It still had a Delhi address on the outside and no wheels but Gerry said it didn't matter; they were sending a car for him anyway. Once we filled the suitcase, I realized how little of him there had been in our apartment: just some clothes, his toiletries, his pillowcase, and the shoes that lined the mat outside. Everything else was mine. I cried even though it wasn't very manly and he laughed, touched my face, and kissed me full on the mouth, leaving me with a hole I couldn't fill with all the HBO left on the TV. I didn't go to work the next day or the day after that. I sat on our couch, rewatching The Wire, while the world outside disintegrated and our apartment slowly ceased to look and feel like a place Gerry had once lived.

Before he left, Gerry had smuggled home spare parts from the computers at work, things he'd taken out to try to slow down the generation of the lists that would fuel the expulsions. I built the robot out of Gerry's parts, winding the metal to look like his hair, which was messy and curled in ringlets straight up. It was only after he'd packed up for the barracks that I gave the robot Gerry's mustache, which crept over his lips most of the time, even though it was those little hairs that drove me crazy when Gerry kissed me. The rest of the robot came from the apartment, his body built from the hot water heater and his single eye constructed from my old Playskool yellow and blue flashlight. I kept him locked up all day in the darkest part of my apartment. When I opened the door, his light would be on, flashing red or green depending on how he was feeling. I called him Jerry with a J. By the time I opened up the closet door on the night of the first expulsion, we had been alone, the two of us, for 147 days, only ever interrupted by the delivery guy from Hunan Palace, the restaurant where Gerry and I once had our first date.

"The regime relies on you," the Palm Pilot said from my hand as I stood in the closet, Jerry with a J's flashlight lighting up the grey screen, alternating red and green so fast it made me think of Christmas. They'd confiscated all of our other devices and, instead, given us Palm Pilots straight out of the 90s, packed full of regime approved news.

"It is fear that drives the madness," said Jerry with a J. A flash of a green light, then red straight into my eyes.

I looked at the grey screen. On it was a picture, drawn with the stylus, of the dumpster behind my apartment building. Then as if it were happening on a piece of paper in front of me, someone squiggled out "meet me @ 7:30." It had been months since I'd seen his handwriting.

"What do you think?" I asked Jerry with a J. "Is it really him?"

"The risk is infinite," he said, flashing red, green, and then red again. The past few months it had been our game: I'd ask him to assess the risk of everything I did and he'd respond with his calculation.

"Minor," he'd said when I'd first asked about the risk of slipping on the bathtub and cracking my head open when I showered.

"Miniscule," he'd said when I asked him about the prospect of causing a fire in the kitchen. "Just watch your burners."

But when I asked him about going outside, he always said the same thing.

"Every situation I compute ends in chaos."

That was fine with me. Every time I tried to walk out the door, I'd get dizzy, my heart beating too fast. Too risky, my mind said and Jerry with a J agreed.

I stood there looking at the handwriting on the screen, filling up with something awful and wonderful at once.

"It's him," I said, "It has to be."

"The risk is infinite," Jerry with a J said. This time, he paused and made a noise like swallowing again, a gargle in the back of the water pipe that was his throat. "That does not mean you should not go," he said. I looked at the flashlight on top of his head. It switched from green to red and back again.

How could something have infinite risk and still be worth it? I thought of Gerry with a G, his too long mustache, and the pile of unkempt curls on top of his head. I looked at my Palm Pilot. The screen had gone to sleep. It showed nothing but the time, 7:28.

My heart still beat too fast, my head already light, but something else was dragging me forward, across the line between outside and in. I stood up and said nothing.

"Be careful," Jerry with a J said.

***

I left the cushiony darkness of the closet for the uncertainty of the kitchen. Gerry had always been the one to wash the dishes, to sweep the floor, to keep me under control. Without him, the latest of my Hunan Palace stayed on the dishes until there was a film and a smell I didn't like but couldn't stop. I put on my raincoat, zipped it up, raised the the hood over my head, and pulled the strings under my chin until they were tight enough that I knew the hood would stay put, hiding my face from view.

I opened the door as quietly as I could, sliding my feet into my rain boots, just in case, even though the Palm Pilot had said nothing about precipitation. The stairwell was empty and quiet except for the sound of the rain boots slapping against my calves. I moved slowly, trying to minimize the noise. Back when Gerry had been home, we'd hear the neighbors laughing, talking, or singing and we'd make our own noise, as loud as we could, until all there was left to do was laugh at ourselves. Now, as I approached our front door, I listened for the sound of cars driving down what had once been our busy street. There was nothing.

I slid my right foot out the door just after I had opened it, letting my boot hold its weight while I reached my hand into my raincoat pocket and pulled out the Palm Pilot. 7:32, it said. I was already late. I walked down the short flight of stairs to the sidewalk, my boots knocking against my ankles. The path behind the apartment building was hidden behind a row of overgrown bushes. I slipped through, letting the branches rub up against me, pushing back as I moved forward.

It was Gerry, the real one, behind the dumpster. He was thin and his hair had grown long, past his shoulders, his eyes sunken and wild. I wrapped my arms around his waist and felt his hip bones poke into my forearms.

"How is my robot?" Gerry asked.

"Keeps me company," I said.

"What did you end up calling him?" he asked. I let my face slide out of my raincoat hood and pressed my cheek against his beard.

"Come upstairs," I said into his chest. It no longer smelled of cologne but it did smell like Gerry, which was what was important. I wanted to wrap him up in blankets, inhale that scent, and look into his eyes until I had no choice but to blink.

He shook his head. I pulled away until the only thing left touching was our pinkies.

"How do you know the robot is a 'he'?" I asked. I'd never said.

"What else would it be?" he said. We looked straight into each other's eyes as best we could. Even after all these days, I was still a good six inches shorter than he was.

"You're right," I said, "I call him Jerry with J. After all, what would he be without you?"

Gerry's mustache still inched over his upper lip. I thought I saw his slow smile emerge from beneath the overgrown hairs. His eyes looked sad and tired, his hair wild as if he'd just woken up from a long nap. A rat scurried in the bushes, startling us both. I remembered when we'd walked down our block and laughed together at the unexpected rustle of the neighborhood cat in the bushes, a mouse between his teeth. Gerry looked like he couldn't remember how to laugh. I could remember and that seemed worse.

"I'm on the list," he said, looking down at his feet. He was wearing his old pair of Adidas Sambas, green, dirty, and worn at the sides. It had always been a mystery to me why he'd loved those shoes so much. "I'm at the bottom but I'm there."

I felt something itch inside my throat. It was warm outside and the dumpster smelled like rotten food. Flies swirled around the top of it, even as it stood closed, the cover opening up to just an inch of darkness. I wanted to reach toward him and tell him it would all be okay, even though I knew it was a lie.

"I'm sorry," I said, instead. "What will we do now?"

He looked down at me and leaned against the dumpster, wrapping his pin-ky tightly around mine. It was cold, bony, and rough, and yet, there was a clammy warmth to his skin that reminded me of home. I saw him swallow, his Adam's apple bouncing up and down in the moonlight, the smell of gar-bage everywhere. He looked at me, his eyes slick in their cavernous sockets.

"Run," he whispered like it was a question and an answer at once. "They haven't finished building the Northern Wall yet."

That was the one they built to keep us in. The first had been, they said, to keep them out.

Still as I looked at Gerry, the mop on his head more beautiful than I'd re-membered, I thought of Jerry with a J and what he'd said about the infinite risk. It was true. How could you quantify what was outside? It was safer in the darkness of my apartment, the silence of my room, the sloppy solitude of my kitchen.

I shook my head. His pinky slipped away from mine.

"I thought you were dead," I said. But still it wasn't enough.

"They'll come for you someday, too," he said, "Jerry with a J can't stop them."

"Every situation I compute ends in chaos," I said.

Gerry sighed and leaned his head against the dumpster. The smell of gar-bage was everywhere, sweet and foul at once.

"What's the point then," he said, "of staying in your apartment? Why not come with me? At least you won't be alone."

The risk is infinite, my heart said. My mouth said nothing.

"The risk is always infinite," Gerry said in a robot voice, knowing like he always did what was in my head.

"You're right," I said, "and still."

"And still…" He said. He looked at me. His eyes were wet and cold. They didn't look much like I remembered. He reached down and pulled back the hood of my raincoat, my head bare against the night breeze for the first time. He kissed me on the top of my forehead.

"Everything I compute ends in chaos," I said.

"I know," Gerry said. My forehead was warm and wet with his kiss. I no longer smelled the dumpster.

He slid around the corner of the dumpster, his pinky touching mine one last time.

"Stay safe, Fred," he said, and turned away from me. I closed my eyes. I listened for his footsteps but they were soundless. I willed my feet to move. They didn't.

A crack opened up inside of me, just enough to let the chaos in.

Thinning to Fable

by Annie Virginia

Inside the house no snow

No wood of footbridges dark with a staying wet
in a forest black with green
and lore with white

But burning hands under water

A glass of ethanol
on the kitchen table

No direct sunlight

There shouldn't be an owl
wrinkling air into glimmer song
right outside this city window
but there is for the augury
to pick like a splinter
like something delivered

In the house no lake strange
for how it rests without having toiled
how silently it bakes for the sun
wild revival of fish and muck in its dream
of a belly

But shreds of sky
we can see
that still fold out
into the rest
sky and the day last year
when we drank kumquat tea
in a cool dim room
then walked with the sun
through the city
all the way home

A ration of reminders
of backroads the taste of ale
brewed near a harbor the small sound
of pebbles rolled against pebbles
to reveal how massive the mountain
the oaks so many days
we lived without collecting

We used to move around inside
the earth where there was everything

Now we must beg of story
to let us walk to go beyond

How to Ruin Your Morning

By Theresa Okokon

Wake up knowing you have to go to work today. No. It's the NowTimes. So no one has to GO anywhere. You are someone, but you are also no one, just like everybody else. You don't actually have to GO anywhere, but you do have to go to work today. You have to DO life today. When someone asks "How are you today?" you will have to say something nice like, "I'm well, thank you, how are you?" Wake up knowing this. Wake up dreading this.

Stall. Find the ten-foot charger cord for your cell phone tangled up with you and your bedsheets. Stare at the ceiling of your brand new bedroom. The room is long, shotgun style. Why do they call it shotgun style and not "trajectory of a bullet as it leaves a shotgun" style? Like the ones that killed Breonna. Remind yourself that you promised yourself not to think about murder first thing in the morning.

Find your phone again. What if this cord got wrapped around your neck while you were sleeping? It reminds you of how when your Big Sister was born, the cord that existed to give her life was wrapped around her neck. If the doctors hadn't realized it in time, she could have been born dead, her life force strangling her before her first breath. Remind yourself that you promised yourself not to think about death first thing in the morning.

Continue stalling. Look at your Facebook memories. Scroll. Try to make it regular scrolling, not doom scrolling. Crane your neck to look at the red numbers on your alarm clock. The shotgun style room is already bright with sunlight, so they don't make a red glow onto your face. It's 7:14am. You promised yourself that you would get out of bed by 7am so you would have time to do yoga this morning. Decide that "by 7am" really means "within the 7 o'clock hour" which means you are still right on time.

Stretch. Notice how when you really put your back into it, it makes your whole body shake. Release a sound. Would you make these sounds if someone else were in bed with you? Maybe for another reason. On the tv show you watched before bed last night, they kept having sex first thing in the morning, and you kept thinking about what it is like to not be bothered by another person's morning breath. You are bothered by your own morning breath, so you have never enjoyed morning sex—smelling your own breath as you orgasm. La petite mort. Remind yourself that you promised yourself not to think about death first thing in the morning.

Make your body perpendicular to the bed. Your knees on the edge, your belly down, your feet pointing to the ground. Tip. Tip. Tip until your toes touch the ground. You did it! You did it. You are out of bed now. Stand up. Stretch again. Stretching is stalling that looks like a healthy thing. Groan. Scratch your belly. Put your hands on your low back and turn your chest up to the ceiling. Release. Ask yourself if this counts as doing yoga?

Smile at your reflection as you walk past the full-length mirror. Tell your reflection that you don't have to shower today. You can wear these panties all day. Maybe you will go to work in nothing but your panties and this cropped Lion King pajama top. Would you dare? Nobody will know. And you are nobody. Just like everybody else. When asked "How are you?" one of your uncles used to respond, "I'm ALIVE!" Until he wasn't. At least you're alive.

Make coffee. Log in.

Sixteen Paris Crossings or
Art in the Time of Crisis

By Trần Vũ Thu-Hằng

When the Museum of Fine Arts re-opened in February 2021, I went
directly to Gallery 232 in the Art of the Americas to see The Daughters of
Edward Darley Boit. It's one of the best-known paintings by John Singer
Sargent, who also painted the murals in the rotunda of the museum. The
eldest Boit daughter is thirteen in this painting, the same age I was when
we escaped Vietnam forty-six years ago. I have four younger sisters and
over my three decades living in Boston, I have looked at the painting many
times, thinking about my sisters and where they have settled across the
United States.

The painting lives between two six-foot-tall, blue-and-white Japanese
vases — the same ones that appear in the portrait. These vases went with
the Boits back and forth between their Paris and Boston homes sixteen
times. It's my goal to cross the Atlantic as many times. Right now, no one
can predict exactly when we can travel safely again, yet I dream of Paris.
My learned response for survival is hope paired with actions. Call it refugee
reflex. I hope for Paris while wearing my masks, doubling them, maintain-
ing social distance, and waiting for the vaccine.

Similar to life in a pandemic, life as a refugee combines fear, loss, and sadness. We refugees cannot be despondent in a crisis. My parents lost their
homes, jobs, and relatives as we fled from Vietnam. My father worked with
the Americans to fight the North Vietnamese Communist government
who had won the war. He would have been executed if we remained in

Vietnam. Normalcy ended for me the day we lunged for the fishing boat.

One thing we never let go of was hope. My parents nearly named their youngest son, born three days after landing in this country, Hope, but an obstetric nurse told them *Hope is a girl's name*. Outside of hope, we clung to work, the relentless bone-tiring struggle to form a new life. It was much like life in a pandemic. There were constantly evolving new requirements.

My parents talked about the future even as we climbed barefoot onto a rescuing merchant vessel, lived in one of the tents in a makeshift camp under the punishing sun in Guam Island, and waited for sponsors in an army barrack turned refugee camp. We rarely took time to mourn the past. We made plans to go to school, learn English, and find jobs once we were on the other side. We dreamed of life on the other side of a refugee camp's fence. I think about this longing for normalcy when my friends tell me *I can't wait to have dinner with you, on the other side of this pandemic.* I want to tell my friends there is no going back to normal, even on the other side.

We work to get to the other side, and then we continue to work when on the other side, for physical survival and emotional stability. During the eighties, only ten years after my resettlement in the U.S., I was an occasional courier, escorting shipments for a transport company called Courier Travel. The company sold twenty-five dollars plane tickets, with short notice, for international travel. The checked luggage allowance was used for their shipments. This was long before September 11 when air travel had a certain innocence. I was desperate to travel out of the United States, even as other refugees, some of them my own relatives in Vietnam, were clamoring to get into nước Mỹ, the beautiful land, as the United States is called in Vietnamese.

Decades after living here, I now understand my desire. I need to feel in control. Unlike my abrupt, involuntary exodus from Vietnam in 1975, now

I can choose the flight, the country, the youth hostel. I can choose when to leave my safe American home and when to come back. I research the destinations, exchange dollars into the local currency, learn a phrase or two of the language, and bring a phrase book with me. I travel to experience the excitement, rather than the dread, of a new language.

I crossed borders to exorcise the traumatic memory of running from my beloved first home, of not speaking the new language, and of not having the possibility of returning home. I want to feel the comfort of being able to go home again, the home I've made here in Boston, the home I was fortunate to have during quarantine. The home where I designed a floral arrangement and recorded one of the free tours that were part of the first ever virtual Art in Bloom for the Museum of Fine Arts.

One day soon, I hope to notch another trip to Paris like the Boit family and their vases. I dream about seeing the City of Light with my four sisters. Hope will sustain me while I work, volunteer, and binge-watch French comedy series until we are all on the other side.

Contributors

Nancy Agabian is the author of *The Fear of Large and Small Nations*, a finalist for the 2016 PEN/Bellwether Prize for Socially-Engaged Fiction and forthcoming from Nauset Press in Fall 2022. She was recently awarded Lambda Literary Foundation's 2021 Jeanne Cordova Prize for Lesbian/Queer Nonfiction. Nancy is a caregiver for her elderly parents in southeastern Massachusetts, where she lives.

Shana R. Ashar lives in Cambridge, MA and has worked at Harvard University since 2006. For the past fifteen years, she has used the university's tuition assistance program to take fiction writing courses at the Harvard Extension School, Cambridge Center for Adult Education, and GrubStreet. "The Robot in the Closet", written in 2017, is her first publication.

Carol Iaciofano Aucoin has contributed book reviews, op-ed columns, and poetry to publications including the *Boston Globe*, WBUR's Arts & Culture, *Pangyrus,* and *Calyx.* She is a co-author of the personal computer anthology *Digital Deli.*

James Burke lives in London, where he writes software and short stories.

Angie Chatman is a freelance writer, editor, and storyteller. Her essays and short stories have been anthologized in *Dine* (Hippocampus Books), and have appeared in *Literary Landscapes, the Rumpus, Blood Orange Review, Hippocampus magazine,* and *fwriction:review.* She has performed stories for The MOTH, the RISK! Podcast, StoryCollider, the World Channel television series Stories from the Stage (WGBH). In 2020 she was nominated for a Pushcart Prize for her essay, "Ode to Poundcake," which appeared online at *Pangyrus.* A Kimbilio Fellow for African American fiction, Angie has received funding from the Virginia Center for the Creative Arts (2020) and Ragdale

(2021). A Chicago native, she lives in the Dorchester neighborhood of Boston with her husband, children, and rescue dog, Lizzie.

Felicia Sanzari Chernesky is a longtime editor, slowly publishing poet, and author of six picture books, including *From Apple Trees to Cider, Please!* (Albert Whitman). In 2018 she left the masthead to help writers share their ideas in print. Her work has received a 2020 Allen Ginsberg Poetry Awards honorable mention and 2021 Pushcart and Best Microfiction nominations. She resides in Flemington, New Jersey, and online at www.feliciachernesky.com.

Lindsay Coleman is a high school English teacher in Pennsylvania. This is her first nonfiction essay, as she mostly writes poetry. She is a graduate of the Iowa Writers' Workshop.

Allison A. deFreese is based in the U.S. Pacific Northwest and coordinates multi-lingual literary translation workshops for the Oregon Society of Translators and Interpreters. Her work appears in: *Borderlands, Crazyhorse, Hunger Mountain, La Piccioletta Barca, New England Review,* and *River Heron Review.*

Allaire Diamond's writing has appeared in *Northern Woodlands Magazine, Field Notes* (University of Vermont), *Edible Green Mountains,* and the academic publications *Economic Botany, Journal of Forestry,* and *Reproductive Sciences.* She lives with her family in Jericho, Vermont and works as an ecologist with Vermont Land Trust.

Jeff Friedman's ninth book, *Ashes in Paradise,* will be published by Madhat Press in Fall 2022. Friedman's poems, mini tales and translations have appeared in *American Poetry Review, Poetry, New England Review, Poetry International, Cast-Iron Aeroplanes That Can Actually Fly: Commentaries from 80 American Poets on their Prose Poetry, Flash Fiction Funny, Flash Nonfiction Funny, Fiction International, The New Republic,* and *Best Microfiction 2021* and

2022. He has received numerous awards, including a National Endowment Literature Translation Fellowship in 2016 and two individual Artist Grants from New Hampshire Arts Council. Friedman and noted flash fiction writer Meg Pokrass have co-written a collection of fabulist microfiction, *House of Grana Padano,* that has just been published by Pelekinesis Press in April 2022. poetjefffriedman.com.

Katie Hartsock is the author of *Bed of Impatiens* (Able Muse, 2016). Her poems have appeared in *Poetry, Threepenny Review, 32 Poems, Kenyon Review, Ecotone, New Criterion, Birmingham Poetry Review, Beloit Poetry Journal,* and elsewhere. She teaches at Oakland University in Michigan where she lives with her husband and two young sons. Her second collection, *Wolf Trees,* will be published in 2022 by Able Muse Press.

David Hawkins is a writer, book editor and naturalist from Bristol, England. Recent work appears in *Arc Poetry, Interpreter's House, Magma, Poetry Wales* and *White Review* amongst others. He was awarded second prize in the 2015 UK National Poetry Competition.

Max Heinegg's poems have been nominated for Best of the Net and The Pushcart Prize. He's been a finalist for the poetry prizes of *Crab Creek Review, December Magazine, Cultural Weekly, Cutthroat, Rougarou, Asheville Poetry Review*, the Nazim Hikmet prize and the Joe Bolton Award from *Twyckenham Notes.* His first book, *Good Harbor,* won the inaugural Paul Nemser Prize from Lily Poetry Press and was released in March, 2022. He is also a singer-songwriter and recording artist whose records can be heard at www. maxheinegg.com. He lives and teaches in Medford, MA.

Jacqueline Houton currently copy edits kids' books at Candlewick Press and serves as senior editor at *Boston Art Review.* A former editor of *The Improper Bostonian* and managing editor of *The Phoenix* and *STUFF magazine* (RIP x3), she has written pieces for *The Arts Fuse, Bitch magazine, Boston magazine, Harvard Divinity Bulletin, Publishers Weekly,* and other publications.

"Joy" is the last word of her essay herein — and it's now the middle name of her daughter, born in January 2022.

Cat Huang is a cartoonist, educator, and art director based in the San Francisco bay area, California. She is currently working as a Teaching Artist at Artprof.org, and was formerly an Associate Art Director at Airbnb. She has a forthcoming graphic novel entitled *Nostalgia* (Holiday House 2023). Find more of her work at cathuangart.com

Katherine Huang is a graduate student in genomics and computational biology at UPenn. Her work has appeared in print and online at various places – most recently *West Trestle Review, Sweet Tree Review*, and *The Shore*. When not writing or sciencing, she enjoys dancing and taking naps. You can find her on Twitter @Katabolical.

Mee Ok Icaro is an award-winning literary prose stylist and occasional poet. She is the winner of the inaugural Prufer Poetry Prize, runner-up in the Prairie Schooner Creative Nonfiction Contest, and a finalist for the Scott Merrill Award for poetry as well as the Annie Dillard Award for Creative Nonfiction. Her writing has appeared, or is forthcoming, in the *LA Times, Boston Globe Magazine, Georgia Review, Bennington Review, River Teeth, Witness, Pleiades,* Michael Pollan's *Trips Worth Telling* anthology, and elsewhere. She is also featured in [Un]Well on Netflix and working on a forthcoming memoir. Mee-ok.com

Romana Iorga, originally from Chisinau, Moldova, is the author of two poetry collections in Romanian. Her work in English has appeared or is forthcoming in various journals, including *the New England Review, Salamander, The Nation,* as well as on her poetry blog at clayandbranches.com.

Dani Janae is a poet and journalist living and writing in Pittsburgh, Pennsylvania. She earned her BA in Creative Writing from Allegheny College and returned home to Pittsburgh after graduating. Her poetry deals with the physical and emotional legacy of trauma and addiction, and the intersecting history of her identity as a Black, lesbian, woman. Her work has been published by *Argot Magazine, Pittsburgh Poetry Journal, Palette Poetry, Wax Nine Journal, Levee Magazine, Thin Air Magazine,* and *Slush Pile Magazine.* She is a contributing writer at *Autostraddle.*

Christine Jones is from Cape Cod, MA and is the author of the full-length poetry book, *Girl Without a Shirt* (Finishing Line Press, 2020) and co-editor of the recently released anthology, *Voices Amidst the Virus: Poets Respond to the Pandemic* (Lily Poetry Review Books, 2020). She is also founder/editor-in-chief of Poems2go and an associate editor of *Lily Poetry Review.*

Patricia Spears Jones is an African American poet, anthologist, literary curator, educator and cultural activist who won the 2017 Jackson Poetry Prize from *Poets & Writers.* She is author of *A Lucent Fire: New and Selected Poems* and nine other poetry collections. Her book, *The Beloved Community,* is forthcoming from Copper Canyon Press, Fall 2023. She edited *THINK: Poems for Aretha Franklin's Inauguration Day Hat* and *Ordinary Women: An Anthology of New York City Women Poets.* She has received grants from the NEA, NYFA and awards from the Foundation for Contemporary Art, and fellowships at the Rauschenberg Residency, VCCA, Yaddo, and Camargo Foundation via the BAU Institute, Cassis, France. She was the 2020 Louis D. Rubin Writer-in-Resident at Hollins University. She is organizer of the American Poets Congress and is a Senior Fellow Emeritus of the Black Earth Institute. www.psjones.com

Angie Kang is an illustrator, writer, and designer currently based in San Francisco, CA. Her work has appeared in *The Believer, Narrative, The Offing, The Rumpus,* and other publications. Find more of her work at www.angiekang.net or on instagram @anqiekanq.

Anne Kenner's work has appeared or is forthcoming in *The Gettysburg Review, The Southwest Review, Boulevard, Salmagundi, Columbia Journal,*

Pangyrus and elsewhere, and has twice been recognized as Notable in *The Best American Essays* series. She was a 2016 Fellow at Stanford University's Distinguished Careers Institute, and has been a federal prosecutor, law professor and high school educator.

Maryam Keramaty is working on her first collection of essays. Currently, she is a student at GrubStreet in Boston, where she studies memoir and the personal essay. Her work has been published in *The Manifest-Station*. Her other creative pursuits are nature photography, mixed-media collage, and cooking. Connect with her at www.maryamkeramaty.com

Lindsey Leigh is an illustrator and designer for print and digital media based in Boston, Massachusetts. Her work is inspired by fantasy, folklore, and the natural world. Though her work ranges from the cozy and comforting to the unsettling and spooky, she aims to imbue even the scariest monster with a tender charm.

Julia Lisella is the author of *Always* (WordTech editions), *Terrain* (Word-Tech Editions), and a chapbook, *Love Song Hiroshima* (Finishing Line Press). Her poems are widely anthologized and appear in *Ploughshares, Paterson Literary Review, Alaska Quarterly Review,* and elsewhere. Her collection, *Our Lively Kingdom*, a finalist for the Lauria/Frasca Poetry Prize, will be published by Bordighera Press in fall 2022. She teaches literature and writing at Regis College in Massachusetts.

Rhiannon McCarthy is a queer writer and Wiccan Priestess living in Boston, MA. She learned how to craft a story in the outer wilds of fanfiction, and she is currently inspired by tales of mystery, transformation, and rebirth in Welsh and Irish mythology. Find her on Twitter @thatoneRhiannon. And yes, she was named for the Fleetwood Mac song.

Melissa Mulvihill writes creative non-fiction, fiction, and poetry that speaks to themes related to impermanence, possibility, and living with chronic illness. Recently she has been published with *Tangled Locks Journal, TMP Magazine, Wild Roof Journal, Misery Tourism, Miniskirt Magazine, Wishbone Words,* and *Full House Literary.* She lives and writes from northeast Ohio. You can find her at melissamulvihill.com.

Theresa Okokon is a Wisconsinite in New England. Her essays (and bathroom selfies!) have appeared in *midnight & indigo, ELLE, Cognoscenti,* and Boston.com. Her essay "Me Llamo Theresa," published by *Hippocampus Magazine,* was nominated for a Pushcart Prize in 2020. Find more at theresaokokon.com.

Alexandria Peary serves as New Hampshire Poet Laureate. She is the author of nine books, including *Prolific Moment: Theory and Practice of Mindfulness for Writing* and *Battle of Silicon Valley at Daybreak.* She specializes in mindful writing and gives talks on the topic, including a webcast for NaNoWriMo and a TEDx talk, "How Mindfulness Can Transform the Way You Write." This poem is the title poem in *Battle of Silicon Valley at Daybreak,* published in 2022 by Spuyten Duyvil.

Jonathan Andrew Pérez, Esq. has published poetry at a number of journals and in collections including in: *Poetry Magazine, Ovenbird Poetry, K′in, Waxing & Waning, The Minnesota Review, Into the Void's We Are Antifa Anthology, Allegory Ridge, Frontier Poetry, [PANK]'s Latinx Lit Celebration Issue, Hayden's Ferry Review, Coffin Bell Journal, Guesthouse, Split Lip Magazine, Blood Tree Literature, TRACK//FOUR, Dovecote, Collateral, The Bookend's Review, Hiram, Inklette, Quiddity on NPR, Rise Up Review, River Heron Review, Muse/A Journal, Projector Magazine, Prelude Magazine,* and *Crack the Spine.* Jonathan's first chapbook, *The Cartographer of Crumpled Maps: The Justice Elegies* (2020) was published by Finishing Line Press, and second manuscript, *The Diving: Dark was the Night of Justice,* won the Burnside Review Poetry Prize and was published in spring 2021. He is a criminal justice advocate, civil rights lawyer, professor, and has a day job as a trial attorney.

Meg Pokrass' flash fiction has been widely published and anthologized, most recently in three Norton Anthologies of flash fiction including *Flash Fiction America* (W. W. Norton & Co., 2023) and *The Best Small Fictions 2022*, and has appeared in many hundreds of literary journals. Her seventh collection of flash fiction, *Spinning to Mars*, won the Blue Light Book Award in 2021. Recent writing has appeared in *Washington Square Review, Electric Literature, Waxwing, Big Other,* and *Five Points.* Meg has recently co-written, along with renowned prose poet and microfiction author, Jeff Friedman, a collection of fabulist microfiction, *House of Grana Padano,* that has just been published by Pelekinesis in April, 2022. She resides in Inverness, Scotland, and serves as Co-Founder and Series Co-Editor of the *Best Microfiction* anthology series.

Christopher Porcaro lives in Los Angeles California with his partner, two cats, and a dog. He paints and writes. Work he's produced has been published in: *The William and Mary Review, The Coil, Noble/Gas Qtrly, DumDum Zine, Mangrove Journal,* and *The Citadel.*

Janet Rodriguez is an author, teacher, and editor living in Northern California. In the United States, her work has appeared in *Hobart, Eclectica, The Rumpus, Cloud Women's Quarterly, American River Review,* and *Calaveras Station.* She is the winner of the Bazanella Literary Award for Short Fiction and the Literary Insight for Work in Translation Award, both from CSUS Sacramento in 2017. Rodriguez has also co-authored two memoirs, published in South Africa. Her short stories, essays, and poetry usually deal with themes involving morality in faith communities and the mixed-race experience in a culturally binary world. She holds an MFA from Antioch University, Los Angeles. She is currently Assistant Editor of Interviews at *The Rumpus.* Follow her on Twitter @brazenprincess

Judith Skillman is the author of twenty-one full length collections. Her poems have appeared in *Cimarron Review, Descant, Threepenny Review, Zyzzyva,* and other literary journals. She is the recipient of awards from Academy of American Poets, Artist Trust, and Washington State Arts Commission. Her recent collection is *A Landscaped Garden for the Addict,* Shanti Arts Press. *Subterranean Address—New Selected Poems 2014-2022* is forthcoming from Deerbrook Editions. Skillman teaches for Hugo House. judithskillman.com

SM Stubbs runs a bar in Brooklyn. He is the recipient of a scholarship to Bread Loaf Writers Conference and has been nominated for the Pushcart Prize and Best New Poets. Winner of the 2019 Poetry Prize from *The Freshwater Review,* he was also runner-up in both the *Atticus Review* and *Cagibi Poetry* Prizes in 2019. His work has appeared in *Poetry Northwest, The Normal School, Puerto del Sol, The Pinch, Cherry Tree, Carolina Quarterly, The Bookends Review, Iron Horse Literary Review,* and *New Ohio Review,* among others, with work forthcoming in *december* and *Twyckenham Notes.*

Katie Taylor is a mother of two and professor of education. She studies and writes about how people learn across the lifespan, especially within families. She is from East Tennessee but work opportunities swept her out West to Seattle, Washington where she currently lives. Her work has appeared in *The Bitter Southerner, The Conversation, The Houston Chronicle*, and several academic journals.

Thu-Hằng Tran has been published in *The New York Times, The Boston Globe, Tulsa World* and *The Boston Book Festival Project.* She is a graduate of the GrubStreet Memoir Incubator Program. Thu-Hằng designs flowers and gives tours for the Boston Museum of Fine Arts and the Boston Athenaeum. She has taught flower arranging to students ages 5 to 85. Thu-Hằng is a National D-Licensed soccer coach, a Kripalu Yoga Dance teacher, and the mother of three adult children.

Jessica Treadway's story collection *Infinite Dimensions* will be published in June 2022. Her last collection, *Please Come Back to Me,* received the Flannery O'Connor Award for Short Fiction; she has also published another book of stories and four novels. A resident of Lexington, Mass., she is a Senior Distinguished Writer in Residence at Emerson College in Boston.

Annie Virginia (she/her) is an MFA runaway teaching high school English and Creative Writing in New York City. She received her undergraduate degree in Poetry from Sarah Lawrence College. You may find her most recent work at *Rough Cuts, Brooklyn Poets, The Seventh Wave* in 'Best New Poets 2019', and in *Blue Earth Review* as a runner-up in their annual contest.

Lillo Way's poetry collection, *Lend Me Your Wings*, was released in July 2021 by Shanti Arts Publishing. Her chapbook, *Dubious Moon*, won the Slapering Hol Press Chapbook Contest. Her poems have won the E.E. Cummings Award and a *Florida Review* Editors' Prize. Her writing has appeared in such journals as *New Letters, Poet Lore, Tampa Review, Louisville Review, Poetry East*, and in many anthologies. Way has received grants from the NEA, NY State Council on the Arts, and the Geraldine R. Dodge Foundation for her choreographic work involving poetry. www.lilloway.com

Tim Weed is the author of a fiction collection, *A Field Guide to Murder & Fly Fishing*, and a novel, *Will Poole's Island*. He's the winner of a *Writer's Digest* Popular Fiction Award and his writing has appeared in *Literary Hub, The Millions, Colorado Review,* and other publications. A former National Geographic travel guide Tim is the co-founder of the Cuba Writers Program and teaches in the Newport MFA in Creative Writing.

Amber Wong's work appears in *Fourteen Hills, Craft, under the gum tree, Creative Nonfiction*, and other literary journals and anthologies. An Asian American engineer, she writes about culture, identity, and the riveting minutiae of water and waste treatment, although usually not all in the same essay. She received her MFA in Creative Writing from Lesley University and her bachelor's and master's degrees from Stanford University. More at amberwong.com.

Nick Zelle is a longtime aerial circus artist based in Minneapolis. His critical writing on Contemporary Circus culture can be found on *Cirkus Syd*. Nick holds a B.A. in Comparative Literature from Middlebury College. @ nickzelle

About Pangyrus

Based in the Boston area, Pangyrus is a community of writers, editors, and creative professionals dedicated to art, ideas, and making culture thrive. Pangyrus is about connection. We bring readers to make unexpected connections across a wide range of ideas, genres, and geographies. We also prioritize the publication of new and unexpected voices.

The name's echo of "papyrus" is deliberate: we engage with political and social issues, but edit for writing that will stand the test of time. Our hybrid publishing model — 2-3 posts per week online and 2 print editions a year — allows us the flexibility to publish topical opinion pieces alongside poetry, essays, comics, reviews, and stories.

Index by Author